RISE TO DIVINITY

BRYANT HINKLE

authorHOUSE®

AuthorHouse™
1663 Liberty Drive
Bloomington, IN 47403
www.authorhouse.com
Phone: 1 (800) 839-8640

Published by AuthorHouse 01/31/2017

ISBN: 978-1-5246-6069-7 (sc)
ISBN: 978-1-5246-6076-5 (e)

THIMBLEST

A BULLET OF DEPRESSION

Max is sitting on his knees in his parents' basement in the tool room over the floor drain, contemplating his life and whether or not living is important to him or if the World around him was worth being in at this point. He sees the World as cold and cruel, without love in people's hearts. All he can see is hateful people and the greed that fills men's hearts. People killing and stealing what they please, because they only seek what they desire not what the world needs. The leaders showing no real leadership other then what want more for themselves and their group. Role models teaching their followers the exact wrong message to their followers. And then people just not caring what direction the planet was going.

In despair over these ideas, he takes one last drink from his bottle of wild turkey. He raises the pistol he bought from a gun shop that day holding it to his temple. He thinks one last time about his decision as a tear streams down his cheek, and closing his eyes softly pulls the trigger.

A NEW HOME

Max sees darkness at first. Then, he opens his eyes to an empty room with only a cot. Lying on the bed, he sees a night table next to him with and alarm clock on it. A demon is sitting in a chair next to him. The demon welcomes Max to Hell. Max, without fear, asks the demon why he's not being torn apart. The demon tells Max that the legends of Hell are extremely exaggerated and that he is there to give Max the low down about how Hell works. The demon tells Max that he will work from 8 am to 4 pm.

Max asks curiously, "There are jobs in Hell?"

The demon replies, "Yes, Hell is almost the same as if you were living on Earth. Now, do not interrupt me again." Max sat patiently the rest of the time until the demon was done talking. The demon told Max, his job is to wash windows on a building, three blocks from where he lives. The demon showed Max on a night stand where the building was located with a map and a picture. The demon told Max that after work, he's allowed to do whatever he wants until 9 pm. At that time, his curfew is up and he must return to his apartment. The demon gives Max a yellow wrist band and tells him that he will be free from a demons wrath during his free time before and after work, but during his work hours he is at the demon's mercy. The demon continued his list of rules by telling Max that once a week, he is supposed to report to the basement of the building for his punishment for his sins on Earth. The demon asks if Max understands what he has told him. Max confirms that he was listening and understands the rules.

The demon replies, "Good, then be at the jobs site tomorrow at 8. Go to the front desk of the building and talk to the spirit, and give her this envelope" he hands max an envelope. "She will direct you through the building to where you will be assigned to put on your uniform. One more thing, when you die in Hell, you end up in your cot or the cot at work after a few hours. Once you awake from your death sleep, you will return to work immediately. Do you understand?" Max nods and the demon leaves Max's new apartment in Hell.

It was 5pm when Max walked into his new living room. He saw that his apartment was furnished with a single love seat and a standing lamp in the far corner of the room. The living room led to the kitchen with no door separating it. There was a bathroom next to his bedroom that he noticed was really small compared to what he was used to. Max went to the kitchen to see what food was there, but the only food he found were a bunch of TV dinners that were labeled Devil's Delights. The TV dinners had a crude picture of what he figured was supposed to look like The Devil. So, he read the directions on how to cook the meal and put it in the microwave. While it was cooking, Max noticed that there was only one sink in the tiny kitchen and no oven. Aside from the fridge, the microwave, and the love seat were the only things in his apartment. He didn't even have a window.

After Max finished eating, he decided he was going to go for a walk. Max left the apartment and walked down a long hallway to a single elevator. A man stood there waiting for the elevator to arrive. Max started to make small talk with the man. He said his name was Rupert, and found out that Hell wasn't really as bad as he thought it would be. There were dance clubs, bars, restaurants, grocery stores, movie theaters, everything. Rupert told Max that Hell was one giant city. Max asked Rupert if there was anything outside of Hell. Rupert told Max that Limbo was beyond Hell. Max asked Rupert what Limbo was like. Rupert had never been there.

They talked until the elevator arrived, they got in and pushed the button to the floor they wanted. Max said it was nice to meet Rupert. Max told Rupert "dude I was not expecting this. He demon that was giving me my orientation was wearing a suit, haha." Rupert laughed, and asks Max if he just got to Hell and Max said, "Yes," and explained how he was completely taken off guard by what Hell was really like. Rupert told Max that it took him for a loop too.

The conversation stopped for a few minutes before Max asked what he was in Hell for. Rupert replied that it's not polite to ask that question to people, but he admitted that he was there because he caught his wife having sex with another woman, and eventually left him for the girl taking their kid with. So he shot himself. Rupert obviously felt terrible that he did it. He told Max, "It's after the fact when you finish the sin. Do you realize what you did and how terrible of an act it was? Though

I look back on it now and its kinda ironic. I guess I did cheat on her with a guy so I guess that makes me the pussy, haha."

Max couldn't agree with him because he knew why he did what he did and that Max chose to shoot himself. Rupert then asked what Max did. He told Rupert that he killed himself also. Rupert asked why he did, max said that people are shit and take what they want. Rupert smiled a little and tried to pry into a better reason for why Max killed himself. Max explained "you wouldn't believe how badly things have gotten on earth." Rupert laughed again and told Max that he was not be from earth. "how? You look like me, like a human."

Rupert was still smiling when he tried to explain that everything looks in proportion to whatever species he is most familiar with living as that person in life. "so what I'm trying to say Max is that I'm from your universe, but I am not the same type of being as you. They make us look the same in your eyes as you look the same as me in my eyes. The same goes for the architecture is supposed to look familiar to us as well."

Max rubbed his chin saying, "i think I get it. That's cool though. Do you know why they do that?"

Rupert told Max that it was to keep the peace, "but people still kill each other the same around here. So try not to mess with anyone. But you killed yourself because your planets people are acting like fools? Sorry man but thats kind of silly."

Max agreed with him a little bit saying "well I was drunk and it felt like the right thing to do."

"So it was a statement death?"

"Yes, there was too much crap people were getting away with and I didnt want to be apart of it anymore." Rupert said that he admired that however stupid it was to kill oneself. He came to the conclusion that what Max had done, showed him how very passionate a person he was, and how he felt for the people living on his world.

The elevator doors open to a regular lobby that he would find back on earth. They exit through the lobby doors and Max is a little blown back by the realities of Hell. Rupert sees that, and asks what he's doing at that moment. Max tells him that he was going to walk around Hell for a little bit. Rupert insist that he should come with him. Max asks what he's doing. He tells Max that he was just going to the store down the road. Max didn't even think twice and agreed to join him.

Rupert smiles saying "excellent. This'll help you get to know hell a little better." They continued to make small talk until they got outside, and Max got his first look at what Hell was really like. It was packed with people and demons in suits. Cars filled the streets. Skyscrapers, as tall as the mountains stood in an even line down the streets. The sky was red, but, instead of clouds, there were floating toughs of fire making their way through the sky, mimicking clouds. Even higher in the sky was the sun that glowed a deep red. Max saw that the sun was turning into the moon, as one unit. Max asked Rupert about the sun and why the moon was connected to it. Rupert told Max that the moon is also the sun and it never moves in the sky, only rotates. Max accepted the idea because he couldn't think of any logical explanation for it.

As Rupert led Max through the streets, he noticed the people talking mad shit to the demons. Max asked Rupert why they weren't afraid of the demons. He told Max that people do that on their free time after work because they can't be hurt. Rupert warns Max from doing that though, because of the repercussions. The demons are very spiteful and are good at remembering faces. Max makes a mental note of it. As they are walking to the store, two people are yelling at each other. One of them pulls out a knife and stabs the other. The man that got stabbed falls to the ground and dies. Rupert catches Max's question before he can ask. He tells Max that people are still very violent to each other and have no problem expressing their feelings. Max asks if there is anyone to maintain control of the people. Rupert tells Max that there are no rules for the souls in Hell except for the one rule the demons have for the souls when they wake up in Hell. This made Max very nervous, but

Rupert said "just don't bother anyone. No one here goes out of their way to mess with anyone. People already have a lot on their mind."

They continued down the street to the store. Before they entered the store Max realized that he didn't have any money and asked Rupert if he didn't mind getting him a pop. Rupert told Max that he starts with $100 when he wakes up in Hell. Max starts to check his pockets. Rupert laughs at Max's ignorance and tells him to go to the ATM at the corner of the store. He tells him to hold his yellow bracelet up to the scanner and select the amount of cash he wants. Max gets a little angry with Rupert for laughing at him, but doesn't say anything. When they get into the store Max goes to the ATM and does what Rupert says. The screen tells him his balance and has five touch screen buttons that give an amount of cash he'd like to withdraw. They were in increments of 10. There was a button that let him select a custom amount. Max pulls out $20 and goes to look for a pop.

There were 50 different types of pop in the coolers. They all had the brand name of Devil's Delights. The flavors were very strange and made no sense to him. One flavor was called Pond Fruit Blast, and another was Mountain Tree Root. Max decided to choose by color and selected one that was green with blue bubbles seeping up from the bottom. Max went over to a rack of items; all labeled the same as every other product, Devil's Delight. Max figured out that they were munchies such as chips, snack cakes, and candy. Then, he came across something called Devil's Smoke, which had the same goofy picture of the devil smoking a joint. The bag was the size of a chip bag, but was not clear and he couldn't be sure of what it was. He walked over to Rupert and asked him if this was weed. Rupert said yes, and that they have beer and cigarettes too. Max asked how they could have the same thing if they were possibly from a different planet. Rupert tells Max that the translation works for everything. Max asks how he knows all of this to be true and Rupert tells Max that it's what the souls in Hell have come to understand over the millennium of time that the souls have spent in Hell. Max just shakes his head, not fully understanding what Rupert is talking about and goes to the person at the cash register.

The teen at the cash registers looks like he doesn't want to be there. Max notices the kid's pointed ears. The kid asks if he'd like anything else and Max notices his pointed teeth. Max says he'd like a pack of cigarettes The kid asks, "Menthol or regular?" Max says, regular. The kid grabs a pack and tosses it on the counter. As the kid is getting the total, Max feels compelled to ask the kid how he looks different than the rest of the souls in Hell, but decides that it would be rude. So, he pays the kid and thanks him. The kid seemed genuinly happy for the politness smiling back at Max. Max waits for Rupert to finish his purchases. Once out of the store, Max asks Rupert about the kid at the cash register. He tells Max that he's a half blood. Rupert explains that the half bloods are the offspring of a soul and a demon. He tells Max that it's a rare thing for a soul to have a kid with a demon because demons usually want nothing to do with them. Those that do, usually after sex, leave the female soul with the baby and let the mother raise the child. But, the thing is, when the child is brought into the World, no one accepts it except the mother. So, they do whatever they want and no one says anything to them. They usually get the jobs after the souls get off their shifts and that's how they support themselves. Max feels bad for the half bloods.

After they reached their apartment complex, Rupert asks if he would like to borrow a bowl and a lighter for the cigarettes and weed. Max says yes and thanks him. Rupert takes him to his apartment, which is down the hall from Max. Rupert lets him into his place and he sees how much cool stuff Rupert has. Max asks how he got all the stuff. He tells Max it's from saving up from his job. Max sees the game console in the opening of the entertainment center and points it out to Rupert. He tells Max that it's called The Devil's Box and that it's a game system. Max can't believe how similar Earth is to Hell. Rupert asks if he wants to stay and play it. Max tells Rupert that he'll smoke him up for letting him play with him. Rupert smiles and says, "Agreed." The rest of the night is filled with online shooting games, the Devil's Smoke, and a lot of talk about each others past lives. They got to know each other very well and became friends.

FIRST DAY OF WORK

Max woke up to his alarm clock. He grudgingly got out of bed; still stoned from the potent weed he smoked the night before. He went to the bathroom and took a shower. Once done, he noticed he didn't have any clothes to replace the dirty ones, so he put the same pair on from yesterday. He ate one of the TV dinners in silence and went to work. On his way to work, everyone was in a hurry to get to his or her destination, even the demons.

Max made it to work on time and talked to the person at the front desk. The woman told Max where to go for the locker room and she gave him his locker number and the key for it. As he was walking away to the elevator, a demon entered the building and started to talk to the woman. The woman must have said something wrong because the demon ripped her head off. A man, who Max assumed was a janitor, started to immediately clean up the mess. Before Max got in the elevator, he saw the woman's body turn into black sand. Max got really nervous and pushed the elevator button repeatedly. When the doors finally shut he gave a sigh of relief. Max walked the halls and noticed all the conference rooms and cubicles with both humans and demons occupying them. Once he found the locker rooms, there was a guy waiting for him. The man introduced himself as Donald. The man was very skittish and jumped at the slightest movement or sound. The man told Max what his job was. He was to work with Donald to clean the outside of the windows of the skyscraper on a scaffold. Max opened his locker to find a black jump suite. He quickly put it on and followed Donald to the roof of the building. They got into the scaffold, which looked pretty sturdy. Max was nervous about being up so high. Donald showed Max how to operate the scaffold, which was pretty easy to Max. Once Donald was done teaching Max, he lowered them to the first window and they started to clean it. Many hours passed and before Max knew it, Donald said it was time for brake. He raised the scaffold.

Donald was constantly looking in all directions. Max thought it was kind of weird. Just as they reached the top, a demon flew down and tossed Donald over the edge of the scaffold. He screamed the entire way down, before hitting the ground. Max only watched in horror at the random act of cruelty. He quickly got off the scaffold and went into the building and straight to the locker room. He sat there for a few hours until Donald walked in through a door at the end of the locker room. Max asked where he came from and Donald told him that that's where the beds were located for them if they should die in the work place. Max wanted to know what that was all about. Donald told him that that same demon kills him every day before break. Fear gripped Max. He was worried that the same thing would happen to him. Donald told Max that it was time to get back to work. He follows Donald once again to the roof and got into the scaffold. They continued where they left off cleaning the windows.

Several more hours went by before he started to calm down. It was then that a demon flew down and landed on the scaffold. Both of them looked at the demon. The demon looked at them deciding which one he wanted to kill the most. Donald pointed to Max, fear drowning his face. The demon laughed at them. The demon grabbed Donald and ripped him in half then tossed him over the scaffold. Max watched in horror as the demon looked at him. Max closed his eyes for a few seconds, expecting his heart to be ripped from his chest. But, when he opened his eyes, the demon was nowhere to be found. Max let out a sigh of relief and started to raise the scaffold up. Once at the roof, Max was just getting out of the scaffold when his vision rolled sideways and the worst sensation of pain raced through his head and then, blackness. Max woke up in a white office room with only 10 beds in it. He looked around confused. He got up and noticed he was still in his uniform. The pain he had felt was fresh in his mind.

Max put his hand up and covered his face. He thought about what had happened to him and he came to the conclusion that a demon must have cut off his head when he wasn't looking. He got up and went into the locker room to see Donald waiting for him. Donald told him that he waited for two hours for him to wake up. Donald said that the workday was over and that he can go home. Max took off his uniform and put it in his locker. He noticed that there was no blood on it, but he didn't care about that as much as the fact that he realized that for the rest of eternity he was going to be looking over his shoulder. This thought wouldn't leave his head the entire walk home. A half blood saw how distraught he was and said, "Don't worry bro, its not all that bad" and walked away. It didn't help Max to think any less about his situation.

Once Max got to his apartment, he sat in his love seat for several hours before Rupert knocked on his door. Max got up to let him in. Rupert could tell that he was not feeling the best about. Rupert told him that it's what he has to deal with now. That he made the choice to be there. Max said that he is so open to the elements in the scaffold. that he could be taken out whenever. Rupert told Max that he could get a different job, but that it's difficult to do. Max asked him how he could do that. Rupert told Max that he just has to apply somewhere and wait for a call. Max looked around and noticed that he doesn't even have a phone. He asked Rupert if payday was the same as his. Rupert said that he gets paid every day, right after work. Max asked Rupert if he would take him to a store that sold phones. Rupert said yes. Rupert led Max to a garage under the building. Max followed Rupert to a car that he guessed belonged to him. Rupert unlocked it with the button on his key and they got in. Max thought to himself after watching Rupert unlock the car, that it's all just a horrible façade. The way that Hell is set up is made to look like home back on Earth, but it's just a place of pain brought on by the random mind of a demon's will. He brought up his feelings to Rupert, but Rupert could only try to explain that this is his life is now and if he accepts it for what it is, punishment for his sins, then it'll be a lot easier for him to live in Hell. It didn't help Max feel any better. Rupert apologized for not being able to help him cope with what was going on. Max thanked him for trying and said that it wasn't his fault. It's just going to be difficult for him to live here until he figures out a tactic for controlling his emotions.

Rupert and Max reached a store that resembled Best Buy. Max looked for the cheapest phone he could find. Once he found one, he went to the checkout. There was a half blood working the cash register. Max politely said hi to her and made small talk. She was greatfull for the for the kindness max showed her and gave him a discount. Max thanked her for it and he and Rupert left the store. Once in the car, Max activated the phone. Max thanked Rupert for helping him the last two days. Rupert told him that it's no problem, that he likes helping out new people to Hell. Rupert gave Max his number and Max entered it into his phone. Once they got back to the apartment complex, Rupert asked if he wanted to play some games. Max thanked him but said no. He's going to go look for a new job. Rupert patted him on the back and wished him luck. Max thanked him and went on his way. Max spent his entire free time looking for a job, but came up empty-handed. He went back to his apartment, depressed. He cooked a TV dinner and tried to go to bed after eating, but it was hard for him to fall asleep.

Punishment instead of work

Max woke up to a knock at the door. Max went to the door, and opened it to find a half blood kid. The kid told Max to report to the basement that it was his day for punishment. Max got really worried, and asked the kid where in the basement he should go. The kid told him to push the button in the elevator with the symbol of fire on it. Max acknowledge the kids request, and politely said goodbye to him. The kid smiled, and told Max good luck, and left. Max figured that he didn't have to shower, and instead ate a TV dinner. After which, he left the apartment, and followed the half-blood kids directions.

Rupert was at the elevator waiting with a few other people. Rupert greeted him. Max said hi back. Rupert saw how distress Max was, and inquired about it. Max told him what was going on, and Rupert looked pretty grim along with the other people waiting at the elevator. This didn't make Max feel any better. Rupert didn't sugar coat what was going to happen to him while they waited for the elevator. Max felt sick to his stomach. Once the elevator arrived, and they all got in, Rupert warned Max that he shouldn't say anything. Not a word to the demon destroying his body. Max nodded to Rupert. The other people in the elevator tried to comfort Max, but it was no good. Once the elevator reached the ground floor, everyone wished Max good luck, and left him.

Max couldn't help but get himself worked up. Once he was at the bottom floor, Max entered a red room that was extremely hot. In the middle of the room was a half blood. Max remained true, and greeted the half-blood just as polite as he was to the previous half-bloods. The half-blood smiled, and told him that it was going to be ok. The half-blood asked for Max's name, and then directed him to a door to the right. Max hesitated before opening the door, and then entered. Right when he walked in a demon grabbed him by his head, and tossed him at a wall closing the door after him. Max slowly got up. The room was filled with whips, blades, blunt objects, pliers, and other torture devices. The demon slowly walked towards Max. Max felt fear wrap his head in a dark cloud, so he closed his eyes, and let whatever happen, happen.

The demon worked on Max for the next 7 hours. Brutally destroying his body, and mind. Max didn't open his eyes once, and wished for it to just be over. The demon often called him names telling Max that he was worth nothing. That he was a piece of meat in the cosmic grand scheme. Tears ran down Max's face until he couldn't cry anymore. After the first 2 hours into it. He lost the will to even move, and just lay on the ground. Except when the demon demanded him to get up. After the seventh hour came around, a buzz noise rang in the room. The demon stopped what he was doing grabbed one of the blades from the wall of instruments, and slowly cut Max's head off. He screamed in pain, until his vocal cords were cut and nothing came out anymore. Then darkness took him.

Max woke up in his apartment. He sat up, and looked around. Then he laid back down curling into a ball, and started to cry recounting the pain and humiliation he just went through. He laid there for several hours trying to calm down, but couldn't. He heard a knock at his door. Max didn't get up right away, until he heard it again. He slowly got up, and walked to the door wiping the tears from his eyes. He opened the door to find Rupert holding a bong in one hand and a case of beer that said the devils drank. Rupert asked if he could come in. at first Max said he wanted to be alone, but Rupert insisted. So he let Rupert in.

Rupert sat on the love seat next to Max, and handed him one of the beers. Max opened it, and drank half the beer in a couple of chugs. As Rupert was packing a bowl, he asked how it was. Max didn't answer him. Rupert said that it's a hard life living in Hell. Max, looking distantly, and says "I want to get out of here." Rupert sighed, and tells him that this is his life now. Keeping the same distant face Max started to cry making now sound. Rupert stopped what he was doing, and started to rub his back trying to comfort him. Rupert offers Max the bong. Max graciously accepts it, and takes the biggest hit he's ever taken before. He champs it, and lets it out without coughing then finishes his beer.

They sit in silence for a while, before Rupert asks him if he found another job. Max just shakes his head. Rupert sighs, and says sorry. Then Rupert suggests that he use his laptop. Max looks at him with as big as a smile he can give, despite his current emotional toll, and thanks him taking Rupert's offer. Rupert suggests that they do it after they finish the bowl, and Max couldn't agree more.

After finishing the contents of the bowl, and downing a few more beers, they moved the party of regret to Rupert's apartment. Once in Rupert shows him the laptop. Max gets on, and starts looking for jobs. Rupert gets on his game council, and starts playing it. After several hours of looking, and many beers and bowls later, Max comes across a search for a position. It was listed for limbo; Max asked Rupert what limbo was like. Rupert said that he had never been there, but from what he heard. It was like the rural part of Hell, country settings, Small villages with local stores, and very few demons. Rupert said that it's very hard to get a job out there, though, because it was in such high demand, and there are not a lot of housing out there.

Max took a drink of his beer, and started researching limbo. He saw that he needed money in order to purchase a house in limbo to even get a job. He saw how much it cost, for an average house in limbo. The average asking price was $250,000 for medium sized house, two bedrooms, one bathroom, a decent sized kitchen and living room, even a garage. Max knew that's where he wanted to go. He just had to save the money, and hope he could find a place. Once he was happy with information he found, he went and sat next to Rupert extremely drunk and high. The idea of moving to limbo gave him the smallest sense of hope. Max thanked Rupert for letting him use his laptop, and they played games for the rest of the night.

FALLING INTO A FRIENDSHIP

Several months passed by, with pretty much the same events happening every day. Max wasn't happy, but he accepted it for what it was... punishment. But he had hope. Every day he saved up, only buying what he needed. Rupert and him became very close as friends, and hung out every day. This helped Max forget about how terrible Hell was. Every night they got drunk and high, and played games together.

Max's work was no exception however. He'd get killed multiple times a day, or not at all. It was really random, and hard for Max to figure out how to react to the situations that were constantly unfolding in front of him. After a while he got board of being killed, and accepted his fate. One day even when brake rolled around. He turned to Donald, and said that he was taking a break then jumped of the scaffold. A demon flying overhead, heard what Max said and snatched him before he could hit the ground, setting him on the sidewalk.

The demon told Max that if he wants a brake he has to be alive for it. Max swore to himself as the demon flew away, and was about to walk in the building when two half-bloods that looked about Max's age stopped him. As bad as things were Max still did his best to be polite to all the half-bloods he came across. Max greeted the half-bloods, and asked them how he could help them.

They said that they were watching him jump from the scaffold, and asked him why he did it. Max told them that it was time for his brake. The half-blood started to laugh, and then asked why the demon saved him. Max told them the reason, which made them laugh harder. They said that he was the coolest soul they had ever met, and they introduced themselves. The skinny ones name was Darren, and the husky ones name was tanner. Max commented on their names being normal. They said simply that that's the name there mothers picked for them, Max respected it like a lot of things these days and didn't inquire any further.

They asked if he wanted to hang out after he got off. Max asked if they had to work. They said they didn't care, that they could get a job anywhere. Max smiled at them, and said yea. So they gave Max there numbers, and vice versa. They continued make talk in front of the building Max worked at until his brake was up. Max wished them farewell, and went back to work. Max was pretty excited all through work, and it showed making him a target for the demon flying by the scaffold, but Max didn't care.

After work when Max got home, he called the two half-bloods. They were hanging together so Max only had to call one of them. He asked if they still wanted to come over, they replied "Hell yea." And about 20 minutes after Max called them they were at his door. They greeted each other, and Max let them in. as the two looked around at the lack of stuff that filled Max's apartment, they laughed and asked were all his stuff was. Max told them that he was saving up to move to limbo. They both said good luck finding a place out there, and that they couldn't even find a house out there. Max assured them that he wasn't going to give up hope.

They sat on the love seat as Max went to the kitchen, and got them a beer, but they declined and instead asked for a bottle of pop instead if it was available. Max was surprised asking if they didn't like the taste of the beer. They said that they were stoners, and preferred something with more of a sweetness to it. Max smiled knowing what that's like, and went to his room to grab his weed shoe box and bong. Max set the box on the ground in front of them, and said "i felt the same way before I killed myself." Max went back to the fridge and grabbed three pops.

As they sat there, Max asked them about their past. He asked who their parents were, how old they were, where they worked. Daren said that their dads are assholes, because they left them to be raised by only their moms as almost every demon does. But they loved their moms deeply. Tanner said he was 23, and Darren said he was 22. Max said that he was 23 also.

Max asked if they ended up losing their jobs for coming over. They both laughed and said that they were indeed fired for ditching work. Max laughed too with admiration saying that he couldn't even do that in his mortal life for fear of losing his home, or not being able to eat and so on. Tanner laughed at the idea of not being able to have the freedom to walk away from something as unimportant and trivial as working for someone who doesn't care for you anymore than keeping their business going. Max agreed commenting on that his previous home being nothing but hardship and working for little to nothing, unless you were already among the privileged. Daren said how much of a waist of time that would be to work your whole life to make close to no progress. Max looked down at the floor saying "as life would have it." the half-bloods nodded.

Daren asked why he wanted to go to limbo so bad, that there wasn't much a difference from Hell. That the rules are a little more lax, but there was still punishment. Max said that he just wanted to get away from the city. That he didn't want to see all the people getting killed around him. That if there were less people getting killed infront of him that he'd feel safer. They felt sympathy for him. Max asked what limbo was like. The half-bloods said it was really calm, and quiet, which made Max daydream. Tanner snapped Max out of it, and asked if that's what he really wanted. Max didn't hesitate when he said yes. This made them feel even more sympathy for Max.

Daren said to Max that he knew a place that was for rent in limbo that he was looking at. He said that he could hook him up with the land lords' number. Max stood up not believing what he just said, and asked him if he was for real. Daren sighed knowing that it would be awhile before he could find another place, and said yea. Max, unable to control himself, lunged at Darren hugging and thanking him. Daren was taken off guard, but eventually hugged him back unable to grasp the affection from anyone else but his mom. When Max let go he his eyes were watery from tears. Max asked how much the rent was. Daren told Max that he just had to pay for the initial payment for the house, and that his rent would be paid for by working for the land lord. He told Max that the house was $15,000. Max said that he had $17,000, and started to shake with excitement. Both half-bloods started to smile from his enthusiasm.

Daren pulled out his phone, and gave the number to Max. Max asked if they thought it was a good time to call now. Tanner said "yea dude, go for it." Max called the number immediately. The phone rang a few times before a voice answered the call. The voice sounded sinister, and distant. Max asked the person on the other end if the house was open to move into. The voice asked if he was a soul, half blood, or demon. Max replied that he was a soul. The voice asked if he was willing to work for him without complaining. Max said yes, that he'd do whatever was asked of him. The voice asked how much he had for the down payment. Max told him that he had $17,000 saved up. The voice told Max that he would take $15,000 for the house, and that he had to buy his own bus ticket. Max acknowledge what the voice told him. The voice told Max that he was to leave tomorrow, and gave Max the information regarding the bus he had to take.

The voice continued to give Max orders that he's not to bring anything with him but the close on his back and what he can fit in his pockets. And once he arrived at his new house he's to ride the bike leaning against the fence down the road headed the same way the bus goes after dropping him off, and when he reached the mansion two miles down the road to knock on the front door, and await his presence. Max confirmed his orders. The voice said that he wasn't to be late then hung up the phone.

Max couldn't believe what had just transpired, and he looked at the half bloods for some sort of reaction. They just smiled at him, and said congrats. Max thanked Daren fifty or more times, before he felt like he was being annoying. Daren couldn't help but smile at his own kind deed, it had been the first time he'd ever helped anyone other than another half blood or his mom. He felt like he accomplished more in that moment then in his entire life.

Max sat back down in front of them, and packed a bowl. They smoked and talk casually until they heard a knock at the door. Max got up, and opened the door to see Rupert standing there. Max was so excited he immediately told Rupert the news. Rupert slapped Max on the shoulder, and congratulated him. Max said thank you. Rupert asked how he managed to get a place in limbo. Max let Rupert in, and introduced Darren and tanner. Rupert said hi to them without hate. The two greeted him back. Max told Rupert that Darren was the one that helped him. Rupert thanked Daren for helping Max. Daren said it was no problem. Max said to Darren to not be so modest. Daren smiled, and said thanks. Rupert asked when he was leaving. Max said tomorrow, which bummed Rupert out, but he was still happy for Max.

Rupert suggested that they party at his place, and Max told Darren and tanner that it'd be more entertaining for them. They both said ok, and they moved to Rupert's apartment. The two half-bloods were pretty impressed by Rupert's apartment, and told him. Rupert thanked them. The rest of the night was filled with games, weed, beer, and the half-bloods told them about this pizza place that delivers. Max and Rupert both looked at each other confused thinking that the only food that they could get made for them was at restaurants. Daren said that it's a secret that only the half-bloods know about. Max said perfect, and again thanked the both of them. They both felt pretty good about themselves for helping a complete stranger, and Max didn't let them forget it.

At the end of the night, before everyone left, Max asked the two half-bloods in the hall if they'd come visit him. They looked at him with obvious respect, and said of course. Max feeling compelled, and a little fucked up, hugged them one last time bid them goodnight, and wobbled to his apartment. Max went to bed the happiest he'd been sense he arrived in Hell. He just hoped it was worth it.

THIMBLEST, THE LAND LORD

The bus ride was long and uncomfortable. It took around 6 months to leave Hells city limits, and another 2 months to get to his cottage. Once there, Max realized how remote his place really was. He did exactly what was instructed of him. He brought nothing with him except a pipe, a lighter, and some cigarettes. He took the bike resting in front of the white fence, and rode the bike to the mansion that like he was told by the mysterious voice.

As he rode the bike he took the first real look at his surroundings. There were children everywhere watching him with glowing yellow eyes. They didn't move, only stood and watched which made him feel uncomfortable. Their bodies were a lightish gray and their clothes were black. The scenery around him was a combination of shades of black, gray, and white. It was so quiet that it made him feel calm. Even the old timey bike made no more then a quietly muffled squeaking noise of the chain being pulled by the gears as he peddled.

A few times though the children would run as other silent children with glowing red eyes would chaise them with spears and knifes. The appearance of the children chasing the other children were all black with little bat wings, and small demon horns. Though, they never even noticed Max. They just sprinted after the normal looking children. Max thought it was very odd, and made a note of it.

Once he arrived at the mansion. He set the bike next to the front of the gate, and walked through it. The gate made no noise and moved perfectly as he swung it open. Max walked to the door, and knocked using the door knocker in the middle of the door that was shaped like a sword hilt pointing down. At first it didn't seem like anyone was going to answer the door, but before he could knock again the door opened to a man dressed in a black p-coat that almost touch the ground covering his black pointed boots, with a wide flat hat. The man himself had a long pointed face, with a ridiculous smile that reached from one side of his face to the other. His eyes were solid black ovals. His skin tone was light gray.

The man greeted Max with a formal, giving his name as Thimblest, but calmly eerie voice. Max greeted him back with just as much formality also giving his name. Thimblest said to come inside. Max entered the mansion, and was in immediate awe of the beautiful home. Thimblest said not to gawk, that it wasn't becoming, Max apologized. Max saw that he was floating around instead of walking. Thimblest led Max through the mansion to a study. Thimblest sat down behind a desk, and started by saying that he expects Max to be at the mansion on time at 6 in the morning every day, and that he gets the weekends off. He tells Max that his job is to clean the mansion, and nothing else. Max notices that Thimblests' mouth didn't move when he talked and thought it weird, though, he was too nervous to say ask about it already knowing how hell was. Thimblest continued to say that he is to shower at the mansion before he starts cleaning; sense there is only an outhouse at his cottage. Also that on Wednesdays he is to bring the three pairs of clothes from the cottage to the mansion to be washed, and hands Max four black t-shirts, and four black pairs of wool shorts. Thimblest handed Max a backpack that he figured was for his clothes. Thimblest said that he will be paid and allowance of $20 a day, and told him that the store is 12 miles down the road in the opposite direction of the mansion.

Thimblest got up, and hovered around the desk and told Max to stand up. As Max stood up Thimblest tells him to hold out his wrist with the yellow bracelet. Max did as he was told, and Thimblest removed the bracelet with some scissors, and said he'd get it back if he ever moves to a different house with another landlord or goes back to hell. Thimblest says that he'll take the payment for the house off of the bracelet, and that he will give the rest of the money on it to Max as he wants. As he completely removed the bracelet, Max felt himself shrink to about half his height. Max looked at his hand, and noted that it looked like a teenagers' hand. Thimblest tells Max to change into the clothes he just gave him. Max was about to ask Thimblest about it his sudden change while putting on his new clothes, but Thimblest stopped him saying to save his questions for after he was done.

Thimblest sat back down in his chair, and motioned for Max to do the same. When Max was seated, Thimblest continued to tell the rules. He tells Max that he will be sent home for the day when he feels like he has put in a full day's work, and after that he is free to do what he wants. Also there is no curfew. Thimblest tells Max that the demon children will not bother him unless he interferes with their play time, which he elaborated and said when they are attacking the child souls. Max felt uneasy about that, to just let the children be attacked. Thimblest says his punishment for Max's sins will be given to him randomly throughout the day while he's cleaning the mansion. That he has a bed in the attic that he will spawn on, and that he's to get right back to work when he wakes up. Thimblest didn't give any details about how his punishment that would be carried out.

The last thing that Thimblest tells Max is it's his duty at his cottage to mow his lawn and keep his cottage clean. Thimblest then said that he'd take questions now. Max's first question was whether or not he just turned into a kid. Thimblest nodded, and said the only adult forms in limbo are the demons, that this is a place for demon children to grow up, and for child souls to repent and suffer for their sins in life. Max didn't like the way he said that, and Thimblest caught Max's disgust telling Max that he doesn't like that the kids from the mortal world are here. That he'd rather completely erasing them from existence then have them suffer in limbo. Max couldn't tell if he was attempting to be noble.

Max asks Thimblest if the bike is his. Thimblest replies that the bike is not his, but he is allowed to use it as he wishes and warned Max not brake or loose the bike. Max noted the warning and the tone in which the warnning was delivered. Max asks if there was a phone he could use there at the mansion, or at his cottage. Thimblest said that there was on at his cottage. Max asks if the store down the road sells devil cigarettes. Thimblest says that they do, but he can't smoke in the mansion, however he can smoke outside of the mansion and in his cottage. Max asks if there is anyone else that will be working with him. Thimblest replies that he will be the only one working at the mansion, and that the rest of his tenants live in the village that the store is located. Max's finale question is how his punishment will be carried out. Thimblest tells Max that it'll happen when it happens. Max gets worried, but doesn't say anything else.

Thimblest says to Max once he's sure he's done asking questions, that he'll show him were the cleaning supplies are located. Thimblest leads Max through the mansion to a giant kitchen, and shows him a closet. Inside the closet was a mop sink in the ground next to a floor drain, and a spigot three feet above the drain with a four foot long hose attached to it. There were all sorts of cleaning supplies and rags on a single shelf low enough for Max to reach. There was an old school metal mop bucket. Hanging from the wall was a mop, broom, dust pan, feather duster (made of goose feathers), and two bags. One bag was labeled dirty and the other labeled clean both had wash rags in them.

Thimblest tells Max to get started, but Max asks as polite as possible where he should start. Thimblest says were ever he wants. So Max grabbed the mop and bucket, and starts to fill it putting in powdered soap labeled in bold letters stating its exact use. Thimblest tells Max that the mop is only to be used for tiled floors. Max acknowledges the request, and continues what he's doing. When Max looks over his shoulder again Thimblest is now were to be found, and gives Max a bad vibe. Several hours pass, and Max is dusting a book shelf. Then he feels a painful pinching feeling in his lower back. He turns to see Thimblest holding knife with black blood dripping from it. Thimblest says nothing, only turns and hovers away. Max falls to the ground in agony, and slowly dies. When Max wakes up in a small bed, Thimblest is standing in the door way, and tells him to clean up the blood immediately. He specifies what soap to use to clean up the blood, then leaves. Max is completely confused as to what just happened. Then thinks to himself "is that the punishment I'll be receiving?? Well I guess it's better than being tortured then killed, or being ripped in half, beheaded, tossed off the scaffold...I guess"

Max got out of bed, and found his way to the cleaning closet, and found the soap Thimblest was talking about. As he was filling the bucket Max feels hands slowly start to choke him. Max struggles to get the hands to stop, but is unsuccessful and dies again. This time when Max wakes up Thimblest is next to his bed leaning over him, which scares Max, making him jump backwards in the bed. Thimblest calmly tells Max to clean up the blood from when he was stabbed, then that he's free to go home. Then Thimblest turns and leaves. Max starts to have second thoughts about his new job, but still agrees that it beats Hell by a lot. Max makes his way back to the closet to find the bucket filled and the mop already in the bucket waiting for him. Max shakes his head, and grabbed the mop to move the bucket. As he's turning around Thimblest is standing behind him. Max jumps back dropping the mop. Thimblest catches the mop, and says that he shouldn't shake his head about the kind things he does for him. Max apologists, and grabs the mop from Thimblest. Thimblest tells Max that he's sorry for killing him two times in a row, and gives him his first weeks' pay. Max thanks him awkwardly. Thimblest thanks Max for the work he's done today, and then leaves. Max thinks to himself "what the fuck is going on??"

Max puts the money in his pocket. Max finishes cleaning the puddle of blood, which cleaned up a lot easier than he expected, and went back to the closet to dump the bucket to find the backpack he got from Thimblest with the clothes inside of it. Max grabs the backpack, and puts it on. As Max is leaving he notices Thimblest is no were to be found. Max leaves as quickly as he can while still maintaining a walk. Once outside he passes through the gates and gets on the bike, but before he could leave Thimblest is at the door and tells Max to close the gate. Max quickly closes the gate, and leaves the obscene demon to his business. While Max is riding back to the house the thought of how random and quiet Thimblest is starts to freak him out a little bit. But decides after much debating with himself that despite how creepy his situation is, it's still better then Hell

THE GIRL ACROSS THE STREET

As Max's cottage comes into view, there is a single girl standing on the other side of the street opposite his cottage. She watches him as he leans the bike against the fence where he found it last. He looks at the girl for a few seconds, and then walks over to her. The girl just watches him with her wide glowing yellow eyes. Max asks if he can help her, but she doesn't say anything. He asks if she's hungry, but again says nothing. Max gets confused, and starts to walk away. The girl follows Max through the fence gate and into the cottage without him noticing.

Max gets his first look at the small house, and thinks to himself how perfect it is. The cottage is only one room with the kitchen, a bed in one corner with a single small dresser big enough for the small amount of clothing he has and whatever else he wants to put in it. Next to the bed on the dresser was an antique clock. There was small table, with only two chairs, in the middle of the kitchen with a tiled floor signifying the separation between the kitchen and the rest of the house. There was a small couch facing a widow that was in the front of the house, with a book shelf next to it holding random books about the history of limbo, proper etiquette for all occasions, and random stories about heroism. In the kitchen was a fridge a small counter, with a small sink located in the middle of it underneath another window looking out to the backyard. There was one cabinet above the sink, and two cabinets below the sink. Max opened the cabinets to find dishes and silverware in the one above the sink, and cleaning products, a bucket, and a trash can in the cabinets below the sink. Next to the faucet was a tooth brush in a cup. There was an oven to the left of the counter, which Max assumed was for the TV dinners. Of which he found only three TV dinners in the freezer, and a jug of what he assumed was black milk in the fridge below the freezer. There were two doors other than the one in the front of the house. One that led to the back yard where he saw the, through doors window, led to the outhouse Thimblest was telling him about. And the other door led to the small garage.

Max took one of the TV dinners from the freezer, and put it in the oven. Then lite up a cigarette that he saved from the last stop the bus made before reaching the cottage. Max turned, and choked on the hit of the cigarette when he saw the same girl standing next to the front door. Max swore to himself, and walked over to the girl. Max told the girl not to sneak up on him like that. He asked her how she got in, but the girl said nothing. Max said to the girl that limbo is fucking crazy. The girl still remained silent, and just watched Max. Max just shook his head, asked the girl if she wanted to sit down, but the girl didn't even move. Max thought to himself "oook." He asked the girl if she was hungry, and still nothing.

Max shook his head and started put the close Thimblest gave him in the dresser next to the bed, and set the backpack next the dresser. Then he went to the bookshelf, and grabbed a book titled "how to eat at a formal dinner" Max figured Thimblest put these books in the cottage for him to read, so he better read them. As he read, the girl was really creeping him out, as she just stood in the same spot watching him. She didn't even turn her body towards Max. He tried to ignore her, but he could help but want her to leave. However the timer went off TV dinner before he got the courage to kick her out.

As he pulled the TV dinner out of the oven the girl slowly made her way the Max's side. As he turned he jumped back almost dropping his food. He swore, and held his chest gasping for breath. He said to her to stop doing that, but she made no sign that she understood the request. She only looked at the food. Max asked her if she wanted any of it, but she still said nothing. Max shook his head grabbing a spoon, and sat at the table. The girl followed him to the table. Max got a spoonful and let the girl eat off of it. The girl once finish with the bite looked at Max showing no sign that she was grateful, but he assumed she was. He shared his TV dinner with her to the last bite. Max was still hungry, but decided to save the other TV dinners for tomorrow. He said to the girl that he was going to go to the store tomorrow, and he'd get more food knowing the girl wouldn't reply.

Max continued to read until about 9, before he went to the outhouse. When he came back in the girl was standing in front of the back door when Max walked through it scaring him again. Max swore, and thought to himself never again. He brushed his teeth, and then tried to for 20 minutes to get the girl to leave without pushing her out. But the girl didn't budge. When he tried to physically move her, she started to whimper. Which was unbearably the saddest noise he'd ever heard coming from a person. Max started to feel bad, and decided to let her stay the night. Max set his alarm clock for 5 in the morning, and went to bed thinking about what he got himself into. But still he thought it was better than Hell.

THIMBLE'S MERCY

The next day Max got up at 5. He woke to the girl standing next to his bed, which scared him and made him sweare. He sighed at the odd girl, and got of his bed. He made a TV dinner, and shared it with the girl. Max decided to put on the same dirty clothes from yesterday, and put fresh clothes in the backpack. As he left the cottage, the girl followed Max. Once he got on the bike, and rode away the girl tried to keep up with him. But the girl couldn't run fast enough. Max looked back at the girl running after him. She ran the entire time until he lost sight of her. He felt bad for her, and the devotion she had to follow him.

When Max got to the mansion, he left the bike in the same spot as yesterday. He made sure to shut the gate behind him this time before walking to the door, and knocking. Thimblest answered the door, and said that he didn't have to knock. Thimblest told Max to just come in, and get to work. Max said ok, and came in the house. Thimblest showed Max were the shower was. Along with where the towels were, and were the towels go when he was done using them. Thimblest left Max to his devices. As Max was showering he felt really awarded about being a kid again. He tried not to let it bother him, despite it being hard not to at first glance.

Afterwards, Max got dressed, and went to the cleaning closet. He put his backpack on the hook Thimblest left it on yesterday before he left, and grabbed the window cleaner spray bottle and a rag. The entire day went by without seeing Thimblest, which made Max nervous. Max looked over his shoulder the whole day. About 5 he had just finished mopping the kitchen, when Thimblest rushed Max before he could see him coming. Thimblest pinned Max by the chest, and put a knife to his neck. Max looked in fear at him, with wide eyes. Thimblest held Max there for 5 minutes before letting him go, and telling Max he can go home. Then Thimblest turned, and floated away. Max wiped the blood from his neck, and looked at it. Max still didn't understand Thimblest's logic.

Max got his backpack, and was about to leave, but Thimblest stopped him asking Max if he'd like some coffee before leaving. Max had already had enough of Thimblest's weird nature, and declined Thimblest telling him that he was going to the store when he got home. Thimblest said that it was too bad that he should stay tomorrow. Max told Thimblest, to be polite, that he would. Thimblest said that he was delighted to hear that, and paid him his allowance. Then turned, and left Max at the front door. Max just left, trying not to let Thimblest get to him.

Max rode the bike back to his cottage to see several children standing across the street were the girl had been standing yesterday. They stared at him as he past the children, until ten demon kids started to chase them. The kids scattered with only the sound of their footsteps as they ran, and the same went for the demon kids. Max stopped the bike, and ran to help the kids, but the demons growled fiercely and started to stab him. Max had to stop, and left them alone. He watched horrified as the demons killed 3 of the kids, and continued to hunt the others down beyond Max's sight.

Max held a few of his wounds, the pain wasn't the worst he'd felt. But it was still pretty bad. Max got back on the bike, and grudgingly rode the 12 miles to the small village. All the souls in the village looked like teenagers also, but their eyes didn't glow yellow like the souls that were being chased constantly by the demon kids. However, there were packs of those kids walking the streets aimlessly. So Max assumed they were adults like him that moved to limbo taking on the same body size. A few of the people in the body of kids, said hi to Max as he rode through town, and Max said Hello back. The houses were small even the two story houses.

Max asked one a girl who didn't have glowing yellow eyes where the store was. She pointed in a direction down the street. Max thanked her for the directions. He peddled around for 7 minutes still lost before finding the store. When he found it he walked through the door. The place reminded him of and old west general store from cowboy movies. All the products were behind the "L" shaped counter, on rows of shelves. The only difference was the coolers with the TV dinners, and various pops. The kid on the other side of the counter asked Max how he could help him. Max said that he was going to take a look around for a bit before deciding. The kid said ok, and went back to work stocking items.

Max looked at the selection of TV dinners, and noticed the lack of variety, and how expensive they were as opposed to Hells selection. He grabbed 10 of the dinners, and two pops. He went to the counter, and the kid asked if that'd be all. Max asked for two packs of cigarettes, and some of what Max thought was beef jerky in the glass jar next to the old style cash register, and some devil's smoke. While the kid was manning the till, Max asked why the children souls were so quiet and awkward. The kid said that they never talk, and act very mysterious. When Max asked further, the kid said that he didn't know much more about them. That no one knew why they acted the way they do. Max thought it was strange the lack of information on the lost child souls. Max paid the kid person, and was thankful that Thimblest gave Max a big backpack, because it barley zipped up.

While Max was riding through town heading home, people were running around yelling. Max asked one of the kids what was going on, and she said that the demon kids were coming. Max got scared, and rode the bike through town as quickly as possible. Then the demon kids came out of nowhere, and started killing everyone in sight. When they came close to Max they completely left him alone as if he didn't exist. Max was confused, and left the town hearing the other kid people screaming. Max thought to himself as he rode away "what is going in this place?? Its on its own level of weird. I guess I should be thankful I'm only being killed by Thimblest."

By the time he got home the sun was rotating into the moon, and it was getting dark. He saw that there were several kids standing across the street again. He placed the bike in the usual spot, and turned to the kids that were staring at him. He thought to himself for a few seconds, and decided to ask if they wanted to come inside. They didn't say anything. So Max turned, opened the gate of the fence. The kids all follow Max inside the cottage. As Max was shutting the door it hit one of the kids. Max turned to see a kid staring at him. Max said "really??" he opened the door until the 6 kids were in the house. Max started the oven, and put three of the TV dinners, that were completely thawed from the ride home, in the oven. He put the rest of the TV dinners in the freezer, and put one of the pops in the fridge with the intent of drinking the other one.

Max turned towards the kids that stood in a group that were all staring at him. Max let the weirdness go to the back of his mind, and started reading the book he started yesterday. Once the buzzer went off for the TV dinners, Max was a third of the way done with the book. Max set the book down, and pulled the dinners out of the oven. He went to the table, and said to the kids that the two were for them. The kids huddled around the food, and started to pick at it not even caring about the spoons Max placed next the plastic dish. Max ate his dinner, and watched the kids as they took turns eating the food. Max ate his food before they got half way done with either dish. Max throw the plastic dish away, and went back to his book.

After 20 minutes Max forgot the kids were there until he looked up to see them at the door staring at him. Max figured that meant they wanted to leave. Max got up, and opened the door. He watched as they stopped at the gate. They turned, and looked at Max, waiting for him to open the gate. Max walked to the gate, and opened it. As the kids were walking out, Max saw red glowing eyes in the distance. The kids didn't even notice them. The kids were half way across the street when the demon children started to run after them. The kids panicked, and ran back through the gate. Max shut the gate as the demons got to it. Max took a step back waiting for them to jump the gate, but they stood on the other side passing, and making awful growling noises. Max walked backwards a few steps before turning completely around. He saw the kids standing in front of the door whimpering not taking theirs eyes of the demon children. Max opened the door, and the kids rushed in. Max went back to his book. The kids were at the window whimpering as they watched the demons passing outside. Max got up after a few minutes, and started rubbing their backs giving them encouraging words. They stopped whimpering, and started to stare at Max. Max smiled at them, and went back to his book. A few of the kids continued to look out the window, and the others stared at Max.

Before Max went to bed he looked through the window. The demons were still there passing the street under the single street light. Max shook his head, and thought to himself how fucked up the situation was. Max went to bed. Half of the children were still watching Max, while the others continued to watch out the window. Max watched the kids until he fell asleep. He thought to himself this is still, despite all the strange shit, better then Hell.

The dinner invitation

A year went by, and Max eventually got used to the vibe that limbo put off. He had finished making a mask he started a month ago. He often saved the children often which he started calling them glow sticks because of their eyes and their unwillingness to move unless they had a reason to. He was killed by the demon kids, that he called hunters, a lot for helping them waking up in his bed at the cottage. And he called the adults that moved from hell to limbo normies.

Thimblest would ask Max if he wanted to drink coffee almost every day. He accepted most of the invites, and learned a lot about him. He found out that he didn't agree with the war that heaven and Hell fought for millions of years. Thimblest felt like it was pointless, but god didn't like that he didn't fight for a side. So Thimblest was banished to limbo, were he received land from Lucifer. Max agreed with his point on war, and said that that was one of the reasons why he killed himself, because most people are petty. Thimblest asked what the other reasons were. Max told him exactly how he felt about his home, planet earth, and that it was all the cruelty that was involved in it.

Thimblest told Max how the heaven, Hell, and the mortal universe fit together. Thimblest told Max that inside the rotating moon/sun was where the mortal universe was located, and heaven and Hell formed around the sun/moon like the inside of a sphere. Max could barely understand the concept, but got a general understanding of it. Thimblest told him about the boarders between heaven, Hell, and limbo. Heaven formed the top 76% of the land. Followed by limbo, which was 5%, and Hell was at the bottom 19%. At the very most top point, which was the center of heaven, was God's castle, and Lucifer's giant house was the very bottom in the center of hell.

Max learned a lot through his coffee sessions with Thimblest. That he was a very kind demon. When Max asked him about his kindness, which Max got very close to him, Thimblest said he didn't like hurting people, but it was Lucifer's laws that forced his hand. Thimblest said that he kills people in a way that was, to him, a kind way to murder someone. However he never found joy in it, and reminded Max often that he was sorry for killing him. Max was still creeped out by Thimblest quietly killing him, and the manner in which he would kill him. Thimblest on many occasions would come to the cottage to see if Max was cleaning, and taking care of the yard. Max would always offer Thimblest coffee, of which Max had grown fond of thanks to Thimblest, and Thimblest would say yes and leave before Max finished making it.

Thimblest noticed all the glow sticks that hung around Max's house, and even inside it at times. When Thimblest asked Max about it, Max said to him that he didn't want to see them get hurt. He told Thimblest that he would let them in when the demon kids would show up, and that he would feed them. Thimblest said noting Max's lack of weight, and asked if it was because of him feeding the children. Max said yes, that he would feed them when he had the money to buy enough food for them. Max said that he rarely ate. Thimblest felt sympathy for him, and offered Max lunch when he was at the mansion, which gave them more time to talk. Max was always grateful for the meals.

Max once got the courage up to ask Thimblest why his mouth didn't move when he talked. Thimblest showed Max that he had two mouths. The mouth that was located behind the point that made up the bottom part of his face, and was not visible unless you stood to the side of him, was used for conversation and eating. Were as the mouth he could see on the front of his face that was always smiling and abnormally big was used for eating glow sticks (children) as a way of freeing them from their torment in limbo.

The girl that first showed up in front of Max's cottage was there almost every day. Max asked Thimblest one day when he was checking out the condition of the cottage about the glow stick that kept showing up at his cottage. Thimblest told him that her name was Ashley. Max asked how she was died. Thimblest said that she was playing with her brother throwing a ball, when she ran in front of a car and got hit. Max felt bad for the girl, and made it a point to look after her until she was just naturally living with him in the house.

Daren and Tanner visited Max often. On one occasion they brought one of their half-blood friends over. While they were hanging out, the half-blood, new to Max, said that his place was lame. Daren said that he doesn't even know who he is, and to not talk shit about him. The half-blood continued to complain, until Tanner called him a dick, and told him about the time that Max jumped of the scaffolding. The half-blood laughed, and didn't believe him. Daren confirmed the story. The half-blood agreed that it was a pretty good story, and he backed off of Max. the new half-blood came over pretty often after that day, and they became just as good of friends as Daren and Tanner. Max asked if Daren and Tanner they were still in contact with Rupert. They said they talked to him all the time, so Max always asked them to say hi for him. They said they'd do that for him, and Max was able to keep in contact with Rupert through the half-blood.

One random night at 11, Thimblest knocks on Max's door. Max is a little surprised to see him that late, and asks if he wants some coffee. Thimblest says yes, of course, and sits down at the table. The glow sticks in the house all gathered around Thimblest, and put their hands on his arms. Thimblest grabbed one of them picking her up by the back of her shirt, lifted her high over his head. Max already knew what was going to happen and turns from the scene. Thimblest opens his smiling mouth wide enough to accommodate for the size of the girl, and lowers her into his mouth. Max turns back in time to see the girl smiling as she is let go of. The rest of the glow sticks look sad, and walk to the door. Its the only time Max ever sees the glow sticks have any emotion on their face. Max already knows that Thimblest did it out of pity for girl, and opened the door for the glow sticks to wonder the front yard while still being safe from the hunters. The only glow stick that stays is Ashley, who doesn't take her yellow eyes of Thimblest, but still keeps her distance from him.

Max begins making coffee, and asks how Thimblest can help him. Thimblest tells Max he has some very exciting news. That he's just came from Lucifer's house, and bragged to Lucifer about Max. He told Lucifer how kind Max was to him and the glow sticks. Thimblest said how Lucifer was intrigued by Max, and suggested that he go to a dinner party with him tomorrow at gods' castle. The news shocked Max, and asked Thimblest if he was sure he was talking about him. Thimblest reassured Max that he was indeed the person he was talking about.

Max felt light headed, sat down at the table with his hands on his lap. Max thanked Thimblest, unable to control a smile. Thimblest says that he is to pack his clothes, and come with him tonight, so he could take a shower before they leave. Max did as he was told, and asked Thimblest if he was coming too. Thimblest explained that he was is getting honors for finding Max. Max noted that he said honors, and assumed he was being praised. Thimblest said how important the finding was, meaning Max, and Thimblest has been given a high honor. Thimblest says that he'll be given black angle wings, which was honorable for a demon to receive. Max congratulated Thimblest, and wanted to pat him on the shoulder, but didn't still respectful that he was a demon.

Thimblest told him that they'll be leaving at 5 in the morning, and he'll be waking Max up a 4. Max was a little upset that he wasn't going to be able to sleep much, but didn't say anything. When Max was leaving with Thimblest, Max let the glow sticks in his yard out of the gate. They slowly made their way from the house, often looking back. Ashley walked to the other side of the street preparing to wait for him like she usually does. Max waved to her knowing she wouldn't react. Max got into Thimblest the black antique limo after him. Max saw that the driver was one of the normies form the village in formal dress. The normie said nothing the whole ride except when Max greeted him when he got in the limo.

The car ride was relatively quiet save for small conversations about etiquette, he should use at the dinner. Max told Thimblest that he'd been reading the books in the book shelf next to the couch. Thimblest seemed slightly surprised that Max had been reading the books at all. Once they arrived at the mansion, Thimblest told Max that he is to sleep in his spawn bed. Max nods in compliance, and they parted ways in the mansion. Max does his business in the batheroom he takes his showers in, and goes to bed still over whelmed by the random invite, and most excited to get out of Hell all together.

Dinner with lords, angels, and dad

Thimblest woke Max up at 4 like he said he would. Max took a long time to get out of bed, before Thimblest pushed him into the bathroom warning him not to be late. Max took the warning very seriously, and got ready as fast as he could. Max went to the kitchen to find a normie from the village making eggs and bacon for Thimblest and him. Thimblest had already eaten, and was waiting for Max to sit down. The normie served the food to Max as he sat. Thimblest told Max to hurry, that they needed to be in front of the gate in 10 minutes. Max didn't even finish before Thimblest ushered him to and out the door.

They waited at the gate for 15 minutes before a, front being horse and carriage, and the back half SUV limo, pulled up lightning fast. It stopped equally as fast, in front of Max and Thimblest. The person sitting at the front of the carriage part got down and opened the door for them to get in. Thimblest entered first, follow by Max who thanked the carriage driver. The driver said nothing, and shut the door behind him. A man in a white suit with a black tie and vest told Max, that his driver is stuck up, and not to worry about him. The man was Caucasian, with long black hair, and white pupils, the irises were a deep red, with fire filling in the rest of his eyes. Max looked at the sinister man with awe, and asked if he was Lucifer. He said yes, and called him an idiot, because there were only three of them in the car. Max didn't even mean it like that, but was too sacred to say anything. Lucifer was obviously upset, and let Thimblest know. Thimblest apologized for Max's ignorance. Lucifer smile, and said of "course you are."

Lucifer asked Max if he knew how special it was for him to be in the position he was in. Max politely said yes and how honored he was. Lucifer said that he'd better act like a "fucking" professional. Max said he'd been reading about etiquette. Lucifer said good, that if Max embarrasses him, he was going to put him to work in his home were his real body is, and he'll suffer for the rest of eternity. Max told Lucifer that he understood what was asked of him with obvious fear in his voice.

Lucifer laughed, and called Max a pitiful life form, and still couldn't figure out we his dad loved mortals more than him. Lucifer said that he didn't even care about his dads' project. He huffed about it for several hours, before he fell silent. Afterwards they rode in silence for the next 16 hours.

Max had to go to the bathroom for the last two hours, but was too afraid to ask Lucifer. So he leaned close to Thimblest and whispered that he had to go. Lucifer heard Max, and asked why he didn't ask him. Max looked at the ground, and apologized to Lucifer. Lucifer said no several times, and asked what the reason was that he couldn't ask him. Max, still looking at the floor, told Lucifer that he was scared to ask him for help. Lucifer laughed at his at the position he was in, and asked Max if he wanted to go to the bathroom. Max took a second before saying yes. Lucifer said that Max has a good reason to feel intimidated, and points at the door across the SUV part of the carriage.

Max got up and walked hunched over towards the door. When Max opened and walk through the door, he was surprised at how nice the bathroom was, and how he was able to walk up right. There was a standing shower, a sink, and a toilet, all made of solid gold. The tiles on the floor were obsidian, the tiles on the walls and ceiling, gold squares with diamonds in the middle of the tiles. Max felt that he was way out of place.

Once he was done in the bathroom, and seated back down. He felt brave enough to ask if he could smoke in the carriage. Lucifer laughed, and said that he was finally getting the picture. Lucifer said yes to the cigarettes. While Max was smoking he asked with more courage about what he said about this not being his real body. Lucifer said calmly that the person he sees is a shadow. That he was on house arrest, until God said so. Lucifer huffed, and said how much bullshit it was. Max asked why he and God got into a war, and both Thimblest and Lucifer looked at him.

Thimblest apologized for Max, but Lucifer held up his hand to stop him. Lucifer said to Max never to ask the question to either him, or anyone else at the dinner. Lucifer's tone was frightening, and Max could only nod that he was never going to ask anyone that question. Thimblest again tried to apologies to Lucifer, but he stopped him mid-sentence, and said that that was strike two. Max decided to just sit there quietly until he had to go to the bathroom again.

It was another 36 hours before they made it to heavens gates. Lucifer pointed at a hole in the 30 mile high wall. Lucifer said that he did that with a sneer. Once beyond the massive walls, that took 20 minutes to get through, Max got his first view of heaven. It was beautiful. The buildings were made of white stone, and looked like a cross between Greek architecture, and futuristic European castles. The roads were white and brown cobblestone. Everyone in the streets were partying as hard as they could. Doing whatever they wanted. No one was fighting, nor hating each other for any reason. They just danced, talked, drank, and did whatever drug they felt like. There was no fear of any kind.

Max envied the idea of being free from all the hate and violence, and almost regretted killing himself. However his hate for what the world was, far outweighed his desire to be in heaven. Max noted also that there were different creatures he figured were aliens from the universe, because none of them looked like what an angle was generally portrayed in pictures that he remembered. It wasn't until 40 hours into the ride did he start to see angles. He marveled at their beauty. They glowed a yellow aura, and most of them wore gold and white armor, and carried elegant spears and swords. Their wings were magnificent, and their halos were a gold disc of aura. Lucifer told Max not to stare, obviously jealous of their beauty, and elegance.

It took 56 more hours before Lucifer told Max to take a shower, and put clean clothes on. Once he was finished getting ready, he waited another ten minutes until they finally arrived at Gods front gates to his castle. The wall around the castle was 20 feet high, with a gold gate just as awesome as the gate into heaven. Once past the gate, they drove another

2 hours down a gravel road with trees lining it in perfect sequins. Max finally got to see the castle in all its glory. The castle was the same architecture as the buildings in the rest of heaven. The castle itself was the size of a large city.

An angle opened the door to the carriage, Lucifer got out first, followed by Thimblest, and Max getting out last. It was late evening when they pulled up, and Max was happy to see a normal colored sunset, though it was still the same rotating sun and moon combo. Oh but how beautiful it was seeing the colors he loved to watch as a mortal. Lucifer made his way to the door of the castle with a smug grin with Thimblest and Max following close behind. Max saw that Thimblest was walking, and he asked Thimblest about it. Thimblest said that demons have no powers in heaven, and that he has to walk the entire time. Max wanted to smile at his dilemma, but didn't want to upset Thimblest.

When they were inside, Max saw angles everywhere. An angle came up to the group, and was going to show them which dining hall they were going to eat at. Lucifer huffed, and told the angel by name that he remembers the castle well enough. The angel said that he didn't have to be rude. They got into it for a little bit, calling each other names like daddy's boy, and warmonger. Thimblest stayed completely out of it, and him and Max waited patiently for the argument to be done. After the angel accepted defeat to the argument, and walked away saying how pointless it was that he had to be so mean Thimblest and Max followed Lucifer through the halls. Max could tell that the night was going to be an annoyance as Lucifer was obviously irritated after the fight.

As they walked through the luxurious halls Max was in awe of how original the art work was in comparison to the fact the there was a picture every 2 feet to the next one. The halls themselves were just as magnificent as was the rest of heaven, and it was hard for Max to believe that he was even allowed in to a palace like this. They followed Lucifer for 30 minutes before they reached a dining hall that was at least the size of a football field. The table was, from what Max could tell, white wood that reached almost the full length of the room. There were angles in beautiful robes and garments. There were important souls all around like Gandhi, Martin Luther King Jr., Buddha, and several others. All the people, angels and souls alike, were engaged in conversation, until Lucifer and his group walked in the door. Everyone stopped talking, and stared at them. Max felt really uncomfortable, and wanted to leave. Then angels walked up to Thimblest and started to talk to him, and the conversations continued.

Lucifer told Max to follow him. Max walked with Lucifer leaving Thinmblest over to a group of people circling around a man garbed in beautiful gold and white robes. He looked very serious, but kind. Lucifer budged his way between the people talking, and introduced Max to the noble man. Max politely said Hello to the man. The man said with a voice of authority Hello, and asked Max if he knew who he was. Max, not sure of the man's position, said politely no. The man let out a laugh, and said that he was God. Max bowed immediately feeling the full awe of God's magnitude. God laughed again, and told Max to stand up, that there was no need for that kind of reaction.

God got straight to the point, and told Max that he was there for a reason, and asked if Lucifer had told him why. Max, trying not to upset Lucifer, saying no in a way that he hoped Lucifer wouldn't destroy him later for. God was delighted to hear that, and said that he wanted to be there for the talk. God said that he was going to offer him a deal. God said that he was trying an experiment with a lost soul banished to Hell, which he thinks shouldn't be there. Max asked what kind of experiment. God told him that it was a surprise, and that he would be happy that if he were to except the offer. While Max was thinking about it, Lucifer tried to convince him by saying that he wouldn't spend the rest of eternity in Hell. Max got excited, and asked what he must do. God gave him a white seed, and told Max to consume it before he went to bed when he got back to his house in limbo. Max thought that it was too simple, and asked what the catch was. Lucifer said in a stern voice to remember his place, but God waived his hand at Lucifer. Lucifer looked angry, and Max got nervous quickly accepting the offer. God looked pleased, and just as Max accepted the offer a man joined the group. God introduced him to Max as Jesus.

Max immediately had thousands of questions, and wanted to brag to him how cool it must have been to have all those powers on earth. But before he could ask, Jesus asked him first if he took Gods offer. Max politely said yes. Jesus said that made them brothers. Max asked what he meant by that, but he was in on the surprise too and gave him no hints. When Jesus gave no information, Lucifer told Max to go away. M ax thanked the group for their time and God for inviting him to his home. God bowed his head with a smile and thanked Max for excepting his offer.

Max walked around the giant room for several minutes trying to find Thimblest. Angles would stop Max in his search, and ask if he accepted Gods offer. Max would tell them yes, and they would say how honored he should be. Max felt very special for all the attention, and did his best to not let it go to his head. He found Thimblest deep in conversation with an angle about the fair treatment of souls in Hell. Max waited patiently for Thimblest to notice him, but it was the angle that saw him. The angle asked Max if he accepted Gods offer. Max replied that he did, and the angle, just like the others, told Max that he was very fortunate for the honor. Thimblest was also delighted to hear the news also.

They continued to talk for several hours. People and angles came and went an angle came in from a door in the back, and rang a bell for people to take a seat. Thimblest told Max that they were to sit at the end of the table next to the souls, were as all the angles, God, Jesus, and Lucifer sat at the other end. The food Max ate was amazing, but there was no meat at all, though, it didn't bother Max. The conversations that were happening on Max's end of the table were beyond Max's comprehension, and hard for him to contribute to. Max stuck to talking to Thimblest mostly, and justly so, none of the other souls really wanted to talk to him.

Once dinner was on its last few bites, God asked for Thimblest to his side of the table. When Thimblest reached gods side, he stood up, and formally thanked Thimblest for finding and telling Lucifer about Max. God then placed his hand on Thimble's back, and his hand started to glow white. As god pulled his hand away, wings started to sprout from Thimblest's back. When god had his hand completely away from Thimblest back the wings continued to grow until they reached their full length. Everyone started to applause for Thimblest. Thimblest thanked everyone and bowed slightly. Max could tell that Thimblest felt the same as he did with all the attention.

After he sat back down, the angles served dessert, and the conversations continued. After dessert was finished, many people started to leave. Max heard some loud talking in the distance but didn't acknowledge any of it as he was balls deep in whatever kind of custard he was eating. Then a few moments later Lucifer pulled him out of his chair, and pushed him in the direction of the door. Thimblest asked what was going on, but Lucifer only gave him a look of anger. Thimblest knew and didn't say anything until they got in the carriage.

Once in the carriage Thimblest asked why they had to leave so soon. Lucifer said that his dad was just as stubborn as he remembered, and he doesn't know what he's talking about, among other things. Thimblest tried to calm him down, but Lucifer told him to shut up, and he doesn't know what he's talking about. So Thimblest let it go, leaving Lucifer to brood. The entire ride home was absolute silence. Thimblest knew not to talk to Lucifer when he just got done arguing with his dad, which was often.

They dropped off Max first. While Max was getting out Lucifer stopped him, and told him to hold out his hand. As Max did what he requested Lucifer snatched his hand, and put a black seed in his palm. Lucifer told Max that if he takes Gods seed and not his, that he will know no end to the pain he'll suffer in Hell. Fear gripped Max, as Lucifer pushed him the rest of the way out the carriage. The carriage drove of leaving Max with horror and confusion as he looked at the seed in his hand. When he looked up he saw Ashley standing in her usual spot across the street. Max put the black seed in the same pocket as the other one, and signaled for Ashley to come in. She didn't move until he opened the gate to the fence. Max shut the gate after Ashley got past the entrance. Max held the door for her with the same effect as the gate.

As the two made themselves at home Max put the two seeds on the table, and went to the freezer to get the last TV dinner. As he cooked it he looked at the seeds. He couldn't figure out what Lucifer said was true. Whether he'll stay in Hell, or never come back. He was more terrified of the fact that Lucifer threatened him, but he knew God wouldn't lead him astray either. He thought about these things for several hours until he knew if he didn't get the sleep he'd be no good at work the next day. He took one last look at the seeds, then looked at Ashley, and said to her "should I take both" he giggled at the thought her making any sort of acknowledgment, until she nodded. Max couldn't believe what he just saw. He looked back at the seeds with that new idea. He thought about it, then came to the conclusion. He grabbed both seeds, and some water. Then downed both of them without hesitation set his alarm and went to bed.

JACOB

WAKING UP AGAIN

It was dark when Max woke up. He went to sit up and hit his head on something hard with cushioning on it. He tried to move what was set so low above him, and realized that he was in a confined place. He began to panic, and hit the low surface above him. To his surprise it broke easily. Once he made a hole in the box, dirt started to poor in on him. Confusion ran through his mind. So he started to dig. He dug for 10 minutes before he hit snow, then open air. He looked around in the darkness, and saw that he was in a graveyard. Once he got himself completely out of the hole he looked at the tombstone. It read: "her lies Max Ierick Seihts: he wanted to be buried so he could rise a zombie."

He couldn't understand what was going on. It made no sense to him. Then he understood what the seeds did and were they brought him. Max thought to himself that that'd mean that Lucifer was lying about the black seed unless he were to die again. He thought to himself that he hopes that neither God nor Lucifer would know that he took both seeds. He stood completely up, and recognized the graveyard he was in. he was back in his home town. It was snowing perfectly Max thought as he looked up at the orange light polluted clouds. He decided to walk to his parents' house, and hoped that they were still there.

As he walked the streets he noticed that he wasn't cold at all, that in fact he was at an even temperature. His breath didn't even cling to the air as it should have in the cold. Max also noticed as he passed houses that it must be close to Christmas, because there were lights up everywhere. When he got to his house there were cars on the streets and in the driveway. He noticed one of the cars as his uncles, and he wasn't sure if he wanted to knock or just leave. He waited at for 20 minutes before knocking. It was his aunt that answered the door. She saw him, stuttered something about impossible, then passed out face first on the floor making a thud noise. Max laughed a little at the site.

Someone asked who was at the door so Max walked in closing the door behind him. Not knowing what he should do about his aunt he left her laying on the floor. He heard a voice ask who was here. Max replied "it's me" just as he walked into view of everyone. Many of his family passed out, others started to cry, and the rest ran and embraced him. Max was really uncomfortable with all of the attention. That's when two men said Hello to Max. Everyone stopped talking to Max, and paid attention to the strangers that had been there before Max got there. Max greeted the smiling men, and asked who they were. They told Max that they were half-bloods. Max said that half-bloods have sharp teeth, and pointed ears. One of the men said that they were indeed half-bloods, that the ties they wore signified them as one. Max looked at the ties. The man on left had a black tie, and the one on the right had a blue tie. The man on the right said also that if he should run into one of them to look at the design of tie. That they were exclusive to them, and the color represented their alignment. Max said fine though he didn't really believe them.

The man on the right said that they were there to ease his transition back into earth. Several of Max's family members started to call them out. The man on the left held his hand out, and said that before they get distracted they were to give Max a duffel bag. Max cautiously grabbed the bag, and opened it. Inside was 30 devils delight TV dinners, a carton of devils cigarettes, five bags of devils smokes, and 15 bottles of Max's favorite devils pops, and a brown paper bag with $200 in it, and his mask he made in limbo.

Max looked at the men and said that he believed them. They said excellent, and began telling him that he would be getting an allowance of $200 a month along with a supply of devils products for the time he spends on earths plain. They then handed him a tin of cream, that they said of he ever got a cut, that he was to apply it to the wound and it will heal, but it didn't work if a limb was removed. Max asked them what the point of this was, and that he didn't want to be there. His parents asked Max why he didn't want to be with them. Max said that it was too hard to tell them, and that it shouldn't concern them. They seemed worried, and asked again. Max told them not to ask again, that it would make them sad, and to drop it. After he said that they didn't push the question any further. However they were even sadder than before knowing that there was nothing they could do for him.

Max asked the half-bloods what the reason was why he was there. They said that they never were told why, but to make sure he got everything that he needed. Max sighed, and said that he didn't want to do it. The half-bloods said that he doesn't have a choice, because he ate the seed. Max confessed that he ate both seeds. The half-bloods asked what the other seed was. Max told them, that Lucifer gave him a black seed, and said not to eat gods' seed. The half-bloods looked at each other. Then back at Max with confused and worry on their faces. Max asked what the problem was. They said that they had no idea what could happen to him. That the one seed was supposed to bring him back, and give him powers that a normal person does not have. Max looked at them with distaste, and asked what he's supposed to do with powers. The half-bloods simply said "whatever you want."

Max just shook his head, and said that he wanted to go back to his cottage in limbo. Max's family started to cry knowing that he didn't want to be with them. The half-bloods said that what's done is done and there is no going back. Max grew angry, but before he could argue his point further, the half-bloods said that it was time for them to go. Max attempted to make them stay and answer his questions, but they said that there was nothing more they could do for him.

After the duo left Max turned to his mother and asked his room was still made up for him. They said no that it had been 3 years sense he died, and they turned his room into a guest room. Max asked if he could use the room as his own. They said yes, but asked him if he would stay and talk to them for the night. Max said that he had to clear his head. They said they understood and left him alone. Max went to the guest room, and sat on the bed. The only thing he could think of was "why. Why am I here?? What's the point of this?? I was happy in limbo. Granted it wasn't the best living conditions, but I had a purpose there, to help the children. This isn't fair. He didn't even tell me what I'm supposed to do here. Why also did god give me powers??" he looked at the ceiling, and said quietly so his family didn't hear him "why god??"

BACK ON EARTH

Max for whatever reason couldn't sleep the entire night. He just wasn't tired. He just lay in bed looking at the ceiling. He felt like there had to be a way off the plain. He sighed exhausted from thinking. He rolled over to look at the clock next to the bed. It read 6:47 am. Max rolled back over, and continued to stare at the ceiling. He laid there for another hour before he got hungry, and went down stairs. His parents had already gone to work. He was home by himself. He didn't like it. He made a devils delight, and ate while watching TV. It was the same stuff on the news. The same awful TV shows, and being bitter wasn't helping him cope. So he went to the thing he could always lean on, cartoons. He was glad they didn't change too much. In fact he was a little happy to be watching SpongeBob Squarepants. He laughed a little, and enjoyed himself.

Then breaking news came on and interrupted his program. It was talking about how Max's coffin had been dug up from inside out. Max could help but smirk at how confused they were. The idea of people thinking he was a zombie enlightened him. So he decided to go for a walk to show off a little bit. When he left the house, the sun burned his eyes. He wasn't used to the sun on his old plain. Once his eyes adjusted, he started to walk, still noticing that he wasn't cold only wearing his death suit. He walked downtown, many of the people staring at him, not fully sure if they could believe what they saw. He stopped at a café to get some coffee.

Once in there, people started to stare at him. Max paid no attention to them, and waited in line. Once at the front, the girl working the till stuttered and asked how she could help him. Max said he wanted a black coffee. She said ok, and as she was ringing up the till, she asked what his name was. Max smirked and said his full name. The people in the café all gasped. Max walked over to the side, and waited patiently for his coffee. He saw out of the corner of his eye that someone was taking a video with his phone. Max could only smile, and shake his head. He overheard one girl say something about a zombie. This made Max laugh quietly to himself.

When Max got his coffee the girl was shaking when she handed it to Max. Max thanked her with a smile, and walked out of the door. That was the start of his followers. Max stepped outside of the café, and took his first drink of something other than devils products. Max couldn't taste anything. He didn't even know he was drinking a liquid. He swore, and tossed the coffee into the trash outside of the café. He grew angry at his situation again. He walked around thinking about what he just experienced. It filled him with more hate. As he was walking aimlessly through town he stopped in front of a store, and noticing where he was. Max looked up at the stores name. It was the same gun store that he got the gun he shot himself with. He agreed with himself on what must be done. He walked in the store. The man greeted Max, and then realized who he was. The man said he didn't want any trouble. Max simply asked if he had a gun for under $197.13. The man said yes, and asked what he wanted it for. Max said it was for himself. The man said that he couldn't sell him the gun for that reason. Max yelled at the man that he'd better sell him the gun, or else. The man got nervous, and as scared as the rest of the townsfolk, gave in to Max's demands, and sold Max the gun. The man asked if he was going to hurt anyone. Max said no that he'd never do anything to anyone. The man sighed a little. Max said goodbye and thanks to the man. The man awkwardly said goodbye, and Max was out of the store walking home.

Max had a determined face the whole walk home. When he got to the house his parents were home from work. Max walked in the house, and they greeted him. Max said didn't say anything, and walked to the basement. As Max sat on his knees, he thought how ironic it was that he was there again, about to do the same thing. He took a breath, and held the gun to the side of his temple. He didn't cry this time. He couldn't, it would be pointless, because this is more than a decision. It was something he had to do for himself. He thought before pulling the trigger that he couldn't even enjoy what this plain had to offer him. So there was even less of a point for him to be there. He smiled at gods failure, and pulled the trigger. There was a loud pop from the gun. Max's mother quickly opened the door tears in her eyes, and yelled down in the basement if he was ok. Max sighed, and said yes he was fine. Max got up off the ground, and looked at the floor. There wasn't even any blood on the floor. Feeling defeated he went to the guest room to get the cream the half-bloods gave him. As he went to the room he thought to himself "this is really it... I'm stuck here..."

Radio interview

A month went by, and all Max could do was lay in bed, only getting up to eat when he was hungry. He could only sleep on day out of the week, and he had to be tired to even accomplish a full night. People in the town had gotten frantic. Rumors started about Max, and his coming back from the dead. His parents tried desperately to bring Max from out of his depression. It helped sometimes to talk to his parents, but it usually ended with his parents leaving the room in tears that he was so sad. Max couldn't even cry with them, despite his deep sorrow. A man came to the door one day asking for Max. Max's mom told the man that he could try talking to Max, but it might not work.

So the man went to the guest room, and said hi to Max. Max sat up in the bed, and asked the man what he wanted. The man said there was a lot of buzz about him throughout the town, and that he wanted to do a radio talk show interview with him. Max said he wasn't feeling up to it. The man said that he didn't expect Max to want to do it, that he didn't believe that he was ever dead in the first place. Max frowned, and said that he had no idea where he was coming from. The man laughed, and said he was full of crap. Max stood up and said that he would do the interview. The man smiled, and said smugly good, that he looked forward to talking to him. The man gave Max the day, the time, and directions to the studio, then left. Max sat back on the bed, and thought himself "fine if I'm going to be here then I'll tell the people what it's like on the other side."

When the day came, Max drove his mom's car to the studio. He went inside to find a woman sitting behind a desk. She asked Max what he needed, looking at him with distaste. Max told the woman why he was there. The woman smirked, and told Max with a sarcastic tone where he was supposed to go. Max shrugged the woman off, and follow her directions. When he found the room a man walked up, and told him to go in the room. Max entered the small room. The room had two mics, a table, two chairs opposite each other, and a board with buttons on one side of the table. The man that he talked to was sitting on the side with all the buttons on the board. The man as sarcastic as the woman at the front desk told Max to take a seat. The man introduced himself to Max as Laser the DJ. Max just as sarcastic as Laser said that it was nice to be there.

Once Max sat down Laser introduced Max to the listeners as the man from the grave, then he laughed at his joke and pushed a button that made the sound of a fart. Max calmly shook his head, and asked what it was he wanted. Laser said that his suit was as good as his scam, noting how dirty it was. Max asked again what he wanted from him. Laser said "uh-oh he's getting angry" then pushed a button that made a chicken bucking noise. Max slammed his hand on the metal table making a dent in it, not even realizing his strength until now. Laser said geez, a little scared at Max's strength.

Laser said fine and asked Max, still smug, what heaven was like. Max said it was beautiful, and that everyone was partying none stop, generally having a great time. Laser said of course and asked what the angles were like, and god. Max said that god and the angels were very formal, and that god was very kind, and had a good heart. Laser said "oh boy" and remarked that he's just telling everyone what they want to hear. Max said fine, and told him where he lived the entire time he was there. Laser said oh boy again, and pushed a button that made a goat noise. Max just shook his head, and started to tell him that he lived in Hell.

Max told Laser how terrible it was to wake up every day in Hell knowing that you were going to die for no reason other than a demons enjoyment. How the sky was always red with toughs of fire streaked across the sky. The sounds of constant screaming off in the distance. How scared he was every day. The fact that that was his life now, and he could never come to terms with it. Laser laughed, and asked how the demons were. Max told Laser that the demons wore suits, and they always had this look of "I'm going to destroy your life today" in their eyes. Max told Laser that one day out of the week he had to go to the basement of his apartment complex, and receive his weekly torture. Laser said with even more sarcasm "please enlighten us to that event".

That made Max smile sinisterly, and he told Laser how right when you enter the concrete room they grab you and throw you at a wall. Then they lay into you doing whatever they want. Using whatever tool they deemed appropriate. Keeping you just to the point where you can still live. That the pain they inflicted on him was more brutal then anything the world has to offer. Max said to finish it off still smirking, and with a sinister voice. "All you can do while the demons are having their way is to just lay there. Lay there and hope he's done soon, so he can kill you. That's how horrible Hell is. The pain I felt on a daily bases trumps anything on earth."

Laser just laughed, and pushed another button that made a donkey noise. Max was now the smug one, and continued on about limbo, the children there, the demon children, how much calmer it was. Then Max told laser about Thimblest. Laser made a "phssed" noise, and said how full of crap he was. Max said that's fine that he didn't have to believe him. That Laser would find out for himself. Laser demanded what Max meant by that. Max put his hands on the back of his head smiled, and said "nothing." Laser said whatever, and Max laughed knowing that he got to him. Laser sneered, and said it was time to go to the phones to get comments from listeners.

The first call was a death threat, which Max said that he could come and try to kill him, and that he's already tried to do it himself. Which made the man on the other end of the phone go silent and hang up. The next call asked about Jesus. Max said that Jesus was an inspiration, and a very upbeat guy. That made the caller happy, and she hung up. The next few calls were about Thimblest, and what kind of demon he was. Max explained that Thimblest was very kind, and he never wanted to hurt anyone. Then Max told the listener how the glow sticks would come up to Thimblest hoping that he would eat one of them, to save them from their fate. That made one of the callers start to cry from the thought of the cruelness of the world Max was describing.

Many calls went through, and the entire time Laser was calling Max out on everything. Max ignored Laser for the most part, but the thing that got Max was all the noises he would make with his sound board. Then finally there was a call from a girl. Max immediately thought she sounded cute. The girl very calmly asked Max if he wanted to go on a date. Max said sure and asked for her number. As she was telling him he realized he didn't have a pen, and asked Laser for a pen and paper. Laser laughed at Max and told him to screw off, and to cut it in his arm if it was so important. Max asked calmly if he had a knife. Laser said with a grin "oh god. I have to see this." he pulled out his pocket knife, and handed it to Max. Max flipped the knife open, rolled back his sleeve, and asked again what her number was.

She started to tell Max, and Max nonchalantly started to cut her number into his arm. Laser started to yell what the Hell he was doing. Max simply said "getting her number" Laser commented that there was no blood coming out, and how deep Max was cutting. Before the last number Laser through up, and passed out. Max laugh out loud, and said he got her number. He asked when a good time was to call her.

She said that it's best to call her after 4 pm, because she usually is done with homework at that point. Max asked what school she went to. She said the college in town. Max asked what her name was. She said Zoey. Max got really excited, and asked if he could call her tonight. Zoey calmly said "yea I suppose." Max said great. They talked for I little bit longer then Zoey said she had to go. Max said goodbye to her, then she hung up. Max excitedly got up as Laser was coming to. He asked what happened. Max said with a smile "you through up all over yourself then passed out bro. enjoy the rest of your life." Then Max left the radio station, and he had more followers. It was the first happy thoughts about his coming back. He hoped it would last.

THE FIGHT AT APPLE BEE'S

A week went by, and Max called Zoey every day at 4 pm. He liked her a lot, and it made his parents happy that he wasn't depressed anymore. He got his own phone to call her with. Zoey seemed to like Max too, though she never led on that she did. Max noticed that she was very sarcastic, and calm. But she was a very nice person. She had been going to college for quantum physics at the moment just for a degree, though she was smart enough to do anything. She often said how smart she was in a way that she never got a big head about it. That it just came as second nature to her. He learned that she moved from Canada, to go to school, and she was the one that made the first tablet, making her rich. Max didn't care about her wealth, he was just happy to talk to her. He asked one day if it scared her to know where he came from. She said that it wasn't a problem, that she thought he sounded like a good person, and she like his personality. Max called her out on it jokingly, but she said sternly to never think that that's why she likes him. Max liked her even more for that.

Max asked her one day if she wanted to go on that date she mentioned on the radio. She said yea sure, and they made plans for that night. Max felt silly that she was the one picking him up, sense he still didn't have a car. Once he was in the car, she asked what he was wearing. Max didn't even notice that he was still in his suit. He laughed and said that he forgot he was still wearing it, and said that he just never got around to taking it off. Zoey just shook her head, and started to drive. Max nervously said that she was very cute. She said thanks without even smiling. Max smirked, and said that she didn't seem too enthused to be with him. Zoey said that not much surprises her, so she never really smiles or shows emotions. Max laughed knowing that she's the same person he talks to on the phone, calm, laid back, and monotone.

Max asked where they were going on their date. She said Applebee's. Max said great, but told her that he wouldn't be able to eat. She asked why. Max said that he can't eat normal food. That its like eating air. So he will just be there to get to know her. She said ok. Max laughed again at her stubbornness to show emotion. Zoey asked why he keeps laughing. Max said that she's just hard to get a reaction from. Zoey apologized, but Max said not to. Max said that her car was very nice. Zoey said yea that she enjoyed driving it around. Once they got to the Applebee's. Max tried to run around to open Zoey's door for her, but she was already out. She looked at Max confused. Max tried to say what he was doing for her, Zoey said ok but that he didn't have to help her, and how unnecessary it was. Max just shook his head and smiled feeling stupid for trying. Zoey asked why he was smiling. Max simply said "you" Zoey smiled a little, and Max caught her, and said "ha got ya'" which made Zoey smile a little bigger. Max felt happy to have met her.

As they entered the building, people stared at them. The host seating people nervously asked if it was just the two of them. Zoey said yes, and the host showed them to and empty booth towards the front of the entrance, next to the windows. Their server asked what they wanted to drink. Zoey said a mountain dew, and Max said that he didn't want anything. Zoey and Max started talking about life and what it meant to them. Zoey said that she believed life was beautiful, and a precious gift. That most people can't understand the full emotions that should be given to respect the meaning of life. Max agreed with her, and said how people just don't care about how they find happiness, that they force it with money and material objects. Zoey replied that if they only had a hold of their true feelings, they'd have the passion to live above the norm, but before Max could talk further, these men came into the building. They were loud and rowdy. They demanded that they get a seat now. The host at the front said quickly to follow him. As the men were passing Zoey and Max, Zoey said that they were the exact reason it's so hard to find happiness in the world, that they bring everyone down to their level.

One of the men heard her say that, and stop the group. He asked Zoey to repeat herself. Zoey did without fear. The man got angry and asked if she knew who they were. Zoey said that she didn't care. The man said he was from a gang, and then said to Max that he'd better control his bitch. Max said loudly not to talk about Zoey like that. Before the man could retaliate, his friend said to him that Max was the guy from the news. The man laughed at Max, and called him a bitch. Max looked at Zoey and asked if she wanted to go somewhere else. Zoey asked if he could take them. Max smiled and asked if she was really asking him to beat them up. The man asked if he wanted to die he could try. Max laughed at the man. People pulled out their phones and started to record the conflict. Max looked at Zoey, and said yea for her honor he will.

The group made room for him, and started stretching their arms and necks, then took stances. Max got up from the booth, and the closest man swung at Max. Max grabbed the man's fist, and squeezed. The man's hand crumbled in Max's hand. The man let out a scream. Max couldn't believe how easily the man's bones collapsed under his strength. The man to his left swung, Max barley had to move to dodge it, and he uppercut the man sending him flying into the table behind him with a loud smash. The next man pulled out a knife and tried to stab Max. Showing off, Max let the blade pierce through the middle of his palm. Without flinching he let the man pull the knife out and thrust again. With the direction of the blade, Max letting the man lunge passed him grabbing the man by the top of his pants, and throwing him out of the window. The last man pulled a gun on Max. Max just laughed at the man. The man said he'd do it. Max stepped forward so the barrel was pressed into the middle of his chest, and said "i dont doubt that you wouldn't" the man let three shots go off. Max just stood there unfazed.

He laughed at the man, grabbed the gun from him, and punches the man in the nose breaking his face, and knocking him out.

Everyone was shocked by what just occurred. Max apologized to the people watching, but no one said anything nor did they call the cops. Max looked at Zoey who was completely calm. Surprised a little, Max asked if she was ok. Zoey said she was fine. Max smiled at how calm she was. Calmer than anyone he'd ever met. A man walked up to Max and asked if he was ok. Max turned to see the man was wearing a blue tie that represented him as a half-blood. Max said he was fine, but he thinks they'll call the cops on him. The half-blood said not to worry about it, and suggested that he go to a different restaurant, and told Max about one that he might like. Max asked why he would like it, and the half-blood said that his brother owns it.

Max sighed, and asked Zoey if she wanted to go. Zoey said yea sure. Max smiled and they left casually. When they were in the car, and driving away, Zoey said she had a confession to tell Max. Max asked what it was a little nervous. Zoey said that she wanted to go on a date because she wanted to study him. Max felt broken and betrayed. Max said just under a yell if she even liked him. Zoey calmly said yea. Max looked at her weird, and asked what her deal was. She said again that she doesn't get surprised easily. Max could only shake his head and smile. Max looked out the window in front of him, and asked if she knew were the restaurant was the half-blood was talking about. Zoey said yea, and that it's in down town.

The car ride was pretty quiet. Max had no idea how to gage Zoey. How she would react to things, and what she said about wanting to study him. He couldn't figure out her intentions, and it almost worried him. Zoey looked over at Max for a long time before he noticed. He asked why she wasn't paying attention to the road, more worried about her. She asked if he trusted her. Max said he didn't know. Zoey smiled at the reply, then turned her focus back to the road. Max decided that he didn't think he would ever truly know what she was thinking. When they got to the restaurant, Max didn't help her try to open her door, though he did still open the door to the restaurant for her. She thanked him, and walked in. Max thought the atmosphere was perfect. It reminded him of Thimblest mansion, calm.

A man wearing a black tie that signified that he was a half-blood greeted them and introduced himself as tom. Max and Zoey said their names and greeted him back. Tom said that his brother told him of his coming, and already had a privet table in the back for them. Max was pleased to hear it, and they followed tom back to the table. They sat, and tom asked if they wanted anything to drink. Zoey said a mountain dew, and tom asked which one, Zoey asked what kind they had, and tom said all of them. Zoey said code red. Tom said excellent, and turned to Max. Max said he didn't want anything, and tom said they served devils delights products there. Max immediately said that he would like thorny pin-cushion. Tom said excellent once again, and left.

Zoey asked what a thorny pin-cushion was, and Max said it was basically orange pop, but really sweet. Zoey said ok showing a little surprise. Max was happy for that little bit of emotion. Zoey asked what devils delights products were. Max told her that it's what he ate in Hell and in limbo. Max said that it's the only thing he can eat that makes him full and has any taste. Max said how excited he was to come to a restaurant that served food he could eat, and that half-bloods cook the best food for what it's worth. Zoey said that she'd like to try some, if it was ok with him. Max said sure of course.

Max got serious though and asked how she was planning to study him. Zoey said she was going to monitor him in his everyday living, and when she has sufficient information she was going to ask for a grant from the state. Max asked if she was that serious about him. Zoey said that she's never been so intrigued by anyone or anything on this planet. Max looked at her wired, and asked if that was a complement. Zoey said that it was the biggest complement she could give to any one person. Max asked her again if she liked him, that he wasn't going to help her if she was only interested in how he came to be back on earth. Zoey looked at Max sternly and said that she likes him, and wants to be in a relationship with him. Max said that that wasn't good enough, that he can't trust her because he feels like the only reason she wants to be with him is so she can study him. There was a pause, then Zoey grabbed Max by the caller and pulled him closer, and she kissed him. Max was about to say something, but Zoey put her hand over Max's mouth, and said that she promises that she is not interested in him for what he is, that for what he is was just fortuitous circumstance. Then she let go of Max, and sat back in her seat. Max hovered there for a second before sitting back down. Max decided again that he would never fully understand Zoey, but he was content with that.

He smiled at Zoey, and thanked her. Zoey asked what for. Max said it was because he had a purpose for being on earth now. Zoey smiled a little, which made Max smile. Tom came back with their drinks, and set them in front of their owners. Before Tom could leave Max asked him why his brother had a different color tie, and if it meant that they were different bread. Tom said that he was right, that he was a half-blood demon, and he was adopted by his brother's family who are half-blood angels. Max, being polite didn't ask what happened to his parents, but Zoey wasn't and asked Tom. Tom was a little taken back, but never lost his smile and calm demeanor.

Tom said that his parents died in a plane crash when he was just a boy, and his cousin's family asked his current family if they'd take him in, and the rest is history. Max asked curiously how they could die if they're half-blood. Tom mentioned how curious they were, and they both apologized. Tom said it was of no concern to him. That he needed to tell the history to Max anyways sense he was a permanent residence of earths plain. Max didn't like hearing that, but didn't say anything. Tom told them that they were still mortal, that they've always been around keeping tabs on the humans, making sure things don't get to out of hand. Zoey sarcastically asked what out of hand meant to him. Tom said simply nuclear war, and handed them menus.

Tom asked if there was anything else Max would like to know. Max said not really. Zoey however asked the half-blood, how they would manage to stop nuclear war if it came to it. Tom said that the half-blood alliance is the most powerful organization on the planet. Zoey asked how many of them there were. Max said to Zoey that she should drop it. Tom, however, said to Max that he didn't mind talking to a human, that he liked the conversations he had with them. Zoey seemed pleased to hear that. Tom said that in the world there were only 907,056 of both demon and angel half-bloods. Zoey mentioned how few of them there were. Tom said that they keep themselves low key. That Zoey was the first person to hear this information in over 200 years. Zoey looked at Tom sideways, and asked why her. Tom said it's because of Max. Tom said that the alliance looked her up after the radio incident, and liked her records. Tom said that they, the alliance, considered her to be a possible world leader someday. Zoey was flattered to hear that, but didn't show it. Zoey said that she had one last question. Tom said how he could help her. Zoey asked if she could tell people about the alliance. Tom laughed a little, and said she could try, but she wouldn't get to far. Zoey rubbed her chin, and fell silent staring at Tom. Tom felt a little uneasy with her staring at him, and it showed. Tom said that she was very smart, but that she shouldn't test the alliance. Zoey didn't say anything, only continued to rub her chin.

Tom ignored her, and asked if they wanted a few minutes to look at the menu. Max said yes, and Tom left them. Once he was out of hearing range, Max asked Zoey why she talked to him like that. Zoey was still rubbing her chin. Max asked her again, and Zoey said I'm interested by the thought of them living along side of us. Max asked Zoey if she even understands what kind power they had. Zoey asked him what "kind" of power they had. Max just shook his head at her ignorance and curiosity. He commented that she really is a scientist. Zoey smiled and said that she was indeed a scientist, and that's the reason she was alive was to understand the world in every aspect.

Zoey said that after her conversation with tom, and what she witnessed at apple bee's, her entire world just flipped. Max smiled and said that she was one in a million. Zoey asked if that was a complement, Max replied yes. Max asked her about what she already knew of the world.

She told him about the universe, and what she thinks it's made up of, and its shape. She talked about how the world was today, and how much of a poor state it's really in, and how the few people that want to help in a specific way can't do anything about it, because they feel like they had no power. She talked about how the pollution was tearing the world's ecosystem apart. Max would jump in and share his opinion often making good points which made Zoey happy that they had something in common.

Zoey was about to ask Max something when tom came back. Tom asked if they were ready to order. They both placed their order. Tom said excellent, and left. When tom was away she bluntly asked Max why he killed himself. Max was a little taken back by the question, and said that he didn't really want to say. Zoey said that's fine. Max was taken back even further on how quickly she let go of the question. Max asked Zoey how she can be so simple like that. Zoey said that she just understands how people are, and that she knows when she's not going to get an answer or if she's gone too far. Max smiled and asked why she didn't think she went too far with Tom. Zoey noted that she doesn't fear power. That in fact she likes testing how far she can go with the powerful. Max smiled and shook his head. Max said out loud I'm on a date with a fearless woman. Zoey asked if that was a complement. Max laughed and said yes. Zoey laughed too.

They continued to talk until their food arrived. Zoey asked if she could try some of Max's food. Max said sure, excited to see how a normal person likes the taste of the food he eats. Zoey took a little bit, and her face contorted into a sneer. She spat the food out on her plate, and asked how he could eat the stuff. Max laughed and said that this dish tastes like fajitas to him, and that he ate it all the time in Hell. Zoey smiled at him, and Max pointed it out to her. Zoey commented that she doesn't remember the last time she smiled so much, and thanked Max. Max smiled and said that he was glade he met her. Zoey said she was happy too.

They talked while they ate only stopping to take bites. Once their food was finished Tom brought out dessert and coffee, devils roast for Max, and said that it was on the house. They both thanked Tom, and started eating the dessert. They talked for hours about everything they could think of, until Zoey let out a yawn. Max asked if she was tired. Zoey said yea, and checked her phone to see what time it was. She swore, and said she had to be to class at in 4 hours. Max said that they'd better go then. Max flagged Tom down, though he hated doing that, and asked for their receipt. Tom said that there was no cost that he and Zoey can eat for free there whenever they wanted. Max thanked Tom with great appreciation. Tom said he was happy they had a good time, and asked if he could walk them to the door. Max said yes and they followed Tom to the door. Tom thanked them for the opportunity to meet them. Max thanked Tom for everything, and said to thank his brother for suggesting the place. Tom acknowledges the request and said to have a goodnight.

They left the restaurant and got into Zoey's car. They talked the entire way to Max's parent's house. When they reached the house, they tried to make their time last as long as possible making small talk. They decided to make another date for that Saturday. They paused, and Max said goodnight, and was about to leave when Zoey grabbed Max and kissed him. Max smiled, and Zoey said thanks for being perfect. Max said that that was indeed a complement, and thanked her back for calling the radio station. They looked passionately at each other for a second then Max got out of the car. He watched her drive away, and then went inside. Max had never been this happy before. Not even when before he shot himself. Max finally had a real reason to be back on earth, and decided to make it his reason for being there on that plane.

WITHIN THE YEAR

Over the course of the next year, publicity on Max grew after the video people posted of Max and the gangsters at the Applebee's. There were always people hanging around Max's parent's house, and it made his parents feel uncomfortable. So Zoey and Max agreed to get an apartment together. Zoey and Max fell in love with each other after a few weeks of their first date, and getting the apartment together was a no brainier to them. Once they were moved in together, a half-blood said he carved runes into the outside door frame to keep unwanted people from breaking the door down and coming in. Max looked at the green glowing runes, and asked how they work, but the half-blood said it was a trade secret. Max didn't think anything of it, let them be.

Zoey showed Max her computer gear. Zoey had three screens, two towers, a keyboard for each tower, and two mice. Zoey said she built the towers herself. Max asked what it is she does on her computers. Zoey said with a smirk "to watch the governments and bad guys of course" Max commented often about her fearlessness that being one of those times.

Max often got into fights with the gangs in town. They were constantly trying to get their respect back, but it was a fruitless attempt every time, and Max figured they'd quite soon. But they never did, they only fought harder. The cops were never quick enough to catch Max in the act.

Zoey and Max were so happy to be alive, and to be with each other. Nothing else made sense to them. This was their lives now, they were more than content.

JACOBS LIFE

Jacob woke up to a punch in the face from the kid in his room. Jacob grabbed his face tears filling his eyes. The kid that punched him laughed hysterically at Jacobs's misfortune. The other three boys laughed and said good morning faggot. Then the kids left Jacob alone in the room. Jacob wiped the tears from his eyes, and got out of bed. He got dressed and walked down to the cafeteria in his dorm. Everyone in the cafeteria booed him. Jacob didn't pay any attention to them, and got in line for his food. The boys in front on him asked sarcastically if he sucked any dick to day. Jacob didn't say anything back. The kids laughed and turned back.

Jacob stayed in line, and patiently waited while kids continued to tell him how worthless he was. When Jacob got to the front, and was waiting for the man to give him his food. The man spit all over it. It never used to be that way. The cafeteria man was only able to spit in one spot, but he progressively got better over the years, learning to widen the spray. Jacob grabbed the tray, and walked to the garbage can. All the kids were laughing, and saying that he should eat it. Jacob looked at the food and debated for a few seconds recounting that he ate the spat on food last night for dinner, and decided to skip breakfast despite how delicious it looked today. Which was another thing that cafeteria man got good at was making his food look more appealing than the rest of the kids food. Jacob tossed the tray in the garbage, and everyone started to boo Jacob, and throw food at him. Jacob caught and apple and inspected it, once he found out there were no bites on it he took his own bite, and walked out of the cafeteria.

Jacob left the building to go to his first class. He noted how he wished he had a better p-coat, and how his was full of holes. As he walked towards the building for his first class, a group of boys started to throw snowballs at him. Jacob tried his best to deflect them, but one of them struck him in the cheek just under his eye. Jacob yelped as he realized that it had a rock in it. He started to run for the building, trying desperately to avoid the snowballs.

Once inside he put his hands on his knees and panted for a few minutes. He walked through the empty halls to his first class. The class he hated the most. His teacher hated him with every fiber in her being, and made sure to let Jacob know that by hitting him with books and rulers, throwing pencils at him, calling him every degrading name that came to her head. Jacob walked depressed to his class, and waited in front of the door for as long as he could. Kids started to shuffle in letting Jacob know that he wasn't worth anything to them, but Jacob was used to it now.

As the last kid was in the class room he entered, and the first thing he heard was from the teacher calling him a little faggot. Jacob quietly sat in his chair. He sat there the entire class not paying attention. The teacher often hurting him physically and emotionally to bring him out of his mind, and into the Hell that he lived in. when the bell finally rang, Jacob went to his next class, which he thought didn't suck so much. At least he was in the back of the class, and the teacher simply ignored him. He could usually get away with sleeping through the class, and the teacher made sure that the boys were quiet while they were in class.

The bell rang for lunch, and Jacob was the last one to get to the cafeteria. He waited in line going through the same routing as breakfast. When he got to the front of the line the man sprayed his food with spit. Jacob thought to himself that at least it was tacos, and they were facing away from his mouth, that he could eat what's inside... at least. Jacob ate what he could, and went out for recces. He sat in the cold away from everyone. The boys that live in the same room as him walked up to Jacob. Jacob replied before they could say anything that he didn't want any trouble. The kid that punch Jacob to wake him up saying he didn't care, and the kids started to beat Jacob up. Jacob just lay on the ground trying to protect his face. He started to cry, and the boys made fun of him and continued. When the boys were exhausted they left Jacob crying on the ground calling him a bitch and a faggot. Jacob lay there with no intent of moving, cold in the snow, unable to shiver.

The bell rang, and Jacob laid there for a few minutes more before getting up. Jacob went to his next class, were only the kids got to make fun of him without punishment. The teacher would join in sometimes, making fun of Jacob. The teacher let the boys throw paper balls at him whenever they wanted. Jacob just sat his head resting on his desk, arms crossed in front of his face, his expression of his emptiness written on his face. He didn't make any move to stop the paper balls, nor did he close his eyes when they struck him.

The bell rang, and Jacob went to his last class. He liked this class the best, because it was about the same as the second class, but it was at the end of the day. He slept the entire class until the bell rang. Jacob left the class room, and made his way to the only place he felt safe, a room that no one would ever go in. As he walked through the door he saw the only thing in the room, a dirty bed tucked under a low angled ceiling. He lay on the bed for hours thinking of a way to escape. Then Jacob heard steps approaching the door. The door opened and the cafeteria man came into the room. He looked surprised to see Jacob. He laughed as he cracked his knuckles and closed the door.

When Jacob was able to escape the lunch man's wrath he ran from the room. He ran all the way outside into the dark cold of the winter. He ran as fare as he dared and collapsed in the snow and cried for hours. Once Jacob expended his last tear he laid there in the snow numb to everything, even the cold. He laid there and stared at the dark sky. He thought to himself do I really deserve this for what I am??... I hate myself. He lay there until a voice came over the intercom saying that lights out was in half an hour. Jacob got up and walked to his dormitory.

He got some, what to him, was a clean pair of clothes. He waited for the showers to empty before taking his. Once finished he went back to his room and lay in his bed, trying to go to sleep. The kid that punched that morning flipped Jacob on his back, and told him to eat his spit. Jacob refused and turned his head away from the boy. The boy demanded that he do as he says. Jacob regrettable told the boy to fuck off. The boy looked at Jacob furious. Jacob tried to apologized to the boy, but the boy wouldn't hear Jacob out. He started to beat Jacob up. Jacob tried to get away, but the boy push Jacob off his bed and on to the ground. The boy pinned Jacob to the ground and demanded him to eat his spit. Jacob continued to refuse tears in his eyes. The voice over the intercom said that it was lights out. One of the boys said that he should make Jacob eat his spit tomorrow. The boy got off of Jacob, and agreed with the kid and they went to bed leaving Jacob on the floor. Jacob lay there crying trying not to wake the other boys, until he finally got into his bed. He lay there cold to his feelings, tears still in his eyes, and he thought to himself. A good day in the boys saint Christian boarding school.

Jacobs massacre

Jacob woke in a different world everything was black, and the only person around was his sister. She held him, and Jacob began to cry saying how much he missed her. She ran her hand down the back of Jacobs head showing him as much love as she could. She told him that he's been very strong, and brave. She said how happy she was that he didn't take his life. Jacob said he couldn't, that he knew someday he could get out the school. She said that that's her reason for being there. Jacob pulled away, and asked if she was going to help him. She said the only help she could give him was directions to a man's house. Jacob asked what man. She said that he helped her in her new home many times saving her life from evil. Jacob asked why he would help. She said that there was no guaranty, but that maybe he'll find pity in his situation. Jacob asked if it was even possible for it to happen. That he didn't want to go the distance if there was no hope. She said that there is always hope, and to not give up. Jacob said ok, that he will try. His sister smiled lovingly. She kissed him on the forehead giving him the directions internally. She said to mention a demon named Thimblest to the man when he gets there. Then she said that she had to go. Jacob said "thank you Ashley" she only smiled, and started to fade into the darkness. Jacob held her hand as long as he could.

Jacob woke up suddenly. He sat up and held his face with his hand. He said "Ashley, thank you" the boy that beat him up the night before laughed and commented to the other boys, that Jacob was talking about his dead hoer of a sister. Jacob looked up at the boy. The boy laughed at Jacobs hair asking why it was white, and saying that his dead sister jizzed on his hair. Jacob sat there and thought to himself "why?? Why me?? How could this happen to me?? It doesn't make sense?? What did I do wrong?? No..." the vision of the directions Ashley put into his mind flashed through him, and he broke inside. He thought to himself "it doesn't have to be this way. It doesn't have to be this way... escape. Escape. ESCAPE!!!!"

Jacob started to cry and smile. The boys started to laugh at him. Asking him how he feels knowing that he'll never find happiness. Jacob got up still smiling. The boy started to laugh even harder asking mockingly what he was going to do. The boy turned back the others to talk more shit. Jacob grabbed the only chair in the room, and smashed it over the boys back paralyzing him for life. The other boys took a step back, surprised. They threaten to beat Jacob up. Jacob picked up a leg of the chair that had a point on it. He looked at the other boys still smiling and said "I dare you" the boys took another step back, and started calling him crazy. Jacob said sinisterly "if I'm crazy it's because of you, all of you. You brought this on yourselves'."

Jacob took a step towards them, and they ran out the door. Jacob put the stick down, and changed into some close. Once he was finished changing he picked the stick back up, and left the room. He walked down the hallway. Everyone stared at him scared. None of the other boys attempted to stop Jacob. As Jacob made his way to the front door, the cafeteria man was waiting for him with the boys from his room. The boys saw Jacob first, and pointed him out to the man. The man started to walk towards Jacob, calling him every name he could think of, and how much trouble he's in. Jacob still smiling kept the same pays. When they were close enough to each other the man reached for Jacob. Jacob side stepped the man, and jumped into the air. Jacob saw the mans exposed neck, and plunged the leg of the chair deep into it, then landed on the ground, and continued his same menacing pays. Blood sprayed all over Jacob. Jacob continued to smile. The boys screamed and ran from him.

Jacob walked to the building were his classes were at. He walked the empty halls to his first class. The teacher was sitting at her desk. When she saw him she didn't get up, though she started yelling at him, and calling him names. Jacob looked around still smiling, and saw a meter long wood ruler. He grabbed it ignoring his teachers belittling remarks, and walked over to her. She asked what was all over him. Jacob simply said blood, and hit her across the face with the ruler. The woman went to grab the side of her face, but Jacob caught her hand and brought it down on her desk hard. Then brought down what was left of the ruler, which now had a point, into the woman's hand. The woman screamed in agony. Jacob yelled where her car keys were. The woman didn't answer. Jacob twisted the ruler, and shoved it down harder, and again asked for her car keys. The screamed and pointed at her purse. Jacob left the ruler in her hand, and went to her purse. He dumped the contents of the bag on to her desk, and rummaged through the belongings until he came across what he was looking for. He left, still smiling, the teacher crying in agony, the ruler still in her hand.

He continued out the front doors keeping the same pays as before, and walked to the parking lot next to the building. He found his teachers car and got in. He turned it on backed out hitting the car behind him, and drove for the entrance of the school. There were a group of staff blocking his way, but Jacob still smiling didn't care, and pushed down on the accelerator to pick up speed. The group didn't move thinking Jacob would stop, but Jacob lost his will, and hit as many as he could leaving the school behind. Once on the road Jacob looked back, and started to cry. He thought to himself still smiling "I did it I'm free..."

DRIVING TO A STRANGERS HOUSE

Jacob drove as fast as he could only stopping to steal gas. When he stopped at a gas station he followed a different path then before. Jacob wasn't even sure if he was going the right way. All he had was the sense of direction his sister programmed into his mind, and an image building the man lived in. The cops would almost catch Jacob numerous times, but Jacob was cunning, and would make a turn in the opposite direction to avoid them. The cops were all over the place, but had no idea where Jacob was going. Just that he was headed west. Jacob only had a left over bottle of water with him that his ex-teacher left in the car when he stole it. He rarely slept, and when he did it was only for half an hour.

Fatigue was setting in by the third day, and he almost crashed several times. But he didn't stop going, determined that he'd find salvation from this man that his sister told him about in his dream. It was on the fifth day that he found the apartment complex. He crashed the car in the parking lot, and slowly got out. He made his way through the building and up the stairs. He saw the door that looked like the one his sister showed him, and he knocked as hard as he could. Max opened the door to see the half dead boy.

Max yelled to Zoey "holy shit it's the kid from the news" Zoey said not to let him in, that he might have flees. Jacob said as quick as he could, knowing that he could pass out at any moment, that his sister Ashley sent him, and to mention a demon named Thimblest. Then he collapsed to the ground. Max picked Jacob up, and brought him into the apartment. Zoey asked what he was doing, that he was of no concern to them, and how much of a nuisance he would be considering the police activity it would bring. Max said that Jacob said something about his demon landlord, and wanted to know how he knew about Thimblest.

Zoey looked at Max for a moment and thought about it. Then she looked away and said that he can talk to him when he wakes up, but he can't stay. Max said that it was fine, and brought him into their bedroom, and laid him in the bed. Just as he did, Zoey said not to put him in their bed. Max said "too late." He could hear Zoey huff a little. Max looked at Jacob, and wondered what would compel him to kill 7 people, and drive across the country to find him. Max put his hand on Jacobs head, and said "sleep well. You've earned it."

5'0 COMES FOR JACOB

Max walked back to the living room. Zoey was watching South Park. She asked, without taking her eyes leaving the TV, how he looked. Max said he looked terrible. Like he'd been up the entire drive. Zoey said that she didn't want him to stay long. Max said that if he actually knew Thimblest, then he had an obligation to him. Zoey said that it wasn't their prerogative to help a strange murdering kid live at their house. Max said that Jacob knew about Thimblest, and he at least wanted to know about how he knew him. Zoey said that he could stay until he was rested, and able to shed some light on his situation. Max thanked Zoey, and sat down next to her.

They sat and watched TV for about 15 minutes when they heard a loud bang at the door. They looked at each other, then back at the door. They waited, and then another bang, and another, and another. Max got up, and walked to the door. Max looked through the spy glass to see swat trying to bust down the door with a battering ram. Max turned to Zoey, and said that the cops are here for Jacob. Zoey said whatever, and turned back to the TV. Max smiled at her nonchalant attitude. Max said to stay in the apartment while he talked to them. Zoey said calmly ok. Max waited for the next strike of the battering ram, and noted the ability of the runes the half-blood carved into the door frame, that the door didn't even move when they hit it. Once he heard the door bang again, Max opened the door and poked his head out. The swat all pointed their guns at Max, and told him to freeze. Max smiled, and asked how he could help them.

They said again to freeze, and put his hands in the air. Max just shook his head, and walked out of the door shutting it behind him. As he was walking out a man shot him with a Taser, but Max casually pulled out the hooks tossing them to the floor. Max again asked what they wanted. One of the man said that he was harboring a fugitive. Max asked how they came to that conclusion. Another man mentioned that there was a stolen car crashed outside, and said that they checked the other apartments leaving his as the last one. Max put his hands in the air and shrugged smiling, and said "you caught me." A man grabbed Max's arm and tried to restrain him, but failed.

He asked for help, and another three men attempted to detain Max. Max could only laugh at them. The swat got angry and started to tase and hit Max with their buttons. Max didn't even flinch. He could only laugh at them. They started to yell at him, and punch him. Max figured that it was enough fooling around. He grabbed one of the fists headed for his face, and broke the man's arm, and punched him in the chest sending guy towards the wall making a hole. The other men looked at their fallen friend, and turned back to Max who just shrugged. The men attacked Max, punching and kicking. Max would grab a limb and break it with ease. When there were only three men left they pointed their guns at Max, and demanded that he surrender. Max smiled and calmly said "go for it" the men put about 30 rounds each into Max's chest.

When they stopped they looked shocked as Max didn't even move from the spot he stood in. they took a step back from Max. Max told the swat that Jacob was in his care at the moment, and possibly forever if the situation arises. Then Max asked if they understood. Before they could say anything the pizza guy walked up to Max and asked for $13.56. Max looked at the kid odd, then opened the door to the apartment, and said to Zoey that her calzone was here. Zoey got up from the couch, and walked to the door. They transitioned money for food the man left and Zoey went back into the apartment closing the door behind her. Max shook his head, and asked again if the swat understood what he said. The swat couldn't believe what just transpired, but nodded. Max said good, and went back into the apartment leaving the swat to gather their comrades. Zoey asked how it went. Max said that it went well. Before Zoey could say anything Jacob came into the living room rubbing his eyes, and asked what all the noise was.

JACOBS STORY

Max immediately asked Jacob how he knew about Thimblest. Jacob said that his sister came to him in a dream, and told him about Max, and that he saved his sister several times in her new home. Max asked if Ashley was his sister. Jacob could only nod. Zoey said that he was lying, and heard about Max from TV. Jacob pleaded with her that it was true, and looked at Max and fell to his knees. Jacob started to cry, and beg Max to take care of him that if they sent him back to the boarding school they would tear him apart. Zoey said that he'd be going to Juvenal hall first, and then to prison after he turned 18. Jacob said that he didn't want to kill those people, that he lost control of himself.

Max asked Jacob why he killed those people. Jacob said that they beat him every day sense he's been there. Zoey sat up, and asked what he meant by that. Jacob said that ever sense his mom sent him to the boarding school when he was 10, and every day he was there the other boys would beat him up, the teachers would hit him and call him names. He said that the cafeteria man that served the meals would spit in his food at every breakfast, lunch, and dinner. Max asked why they would do that. Jacob averted his eyes, and said that he didn't want to say, that they would hate him too. Zoey said to go on, and that they wouldn't judge him. Jacob looked at Max, and asked if they were telling the truth. Max nodded, completely serious. Jacob, eyes turned away, said that he was gay. Both Zoey and Max grew angry.

Zoey said to tell them everything. Jacob said he didn't want to, but she insisted. So Jacob decided to start with when his dad died. Jacob said that his dad was a soldier, and died when he was 5. He said that his mom never got over it, and ignored him and his sister. Jacob said that his sister was the closest person to him, and she was the first person to know that he started to like other boys when he was 8. Tears started to fill Jacobs's eyes, as he told them about how he was playing catch with his sister, when he threw the ball into the street, and she got hit by a car. Jacob recounted her dying words to him, and was to not let their mom find out he was attracted to boys. Jacob told them that one day his mom caught him kissing the neighbor kid, and she sent him to a Christian boarding school for boys when he was 10, and shortly after she killed herself. So he was alone in this school, and no one loved him, and hurt him every chance they got.

Jacob held himself letting the story eat his mind away. Max knelt down next to Jacob, and gently pulled his face level with his, and said that everything will be ok. That he would take care of him. Max looked at Zoey with love and concern on his face. She rolled her eyes, and told Jacob he could have half of her calzone. Jacob thanked the both of them, and hugged Max. As Jacob was about to sit down, Zoey said that he had to sit on the floor, because of the blood all over him knowing that it was dry. Jacob didn't care, he could only smile as he ate his half of the calzone. Jacob thought to himself "no spit."

A NEW LIFE

Months passed, and Jacob only stopped smiling when he slept, and even then. Max and Zoey decided that if Jacob was going to live with them he mine as well have his own room. So they moved all of Zoey's computer stuff up into the loft of the apartment, and got Jacob his own bed, clothes, dresser; and lava lamp. They grew very fond of Jacob, and would let him know often how they felt about him. Zoey got him the most ridicules clothes to ware, and some normal clothes. She thought it was funny to dress him up how she wanted. Max would disagree with her, but Jacob didn't care at all, and loved the attention. Zoey made Jacob clean the apartment all the time, even spots that he already cleaned. But Jacob didn't care about that either. It was the happiest Jacob had ever been sense before his sister died.

One day Zoey was playing a shooting game online. Jacob stopped cleaning, and asked what she was doing. Zoey said that she was playing a game system. Jacob asked if he could try. Zoey figured it would be fun to watch a noob play, and gave him the controller. Jacob sat down on the couch, and looked at the controller awkwardly. Zoey didn't tell him how to play, and decided to let him get his ass kicked. Jacob, when he started to play, had no idea what he was doing. But once he figured out the controls, he was a wiz, and for every minute that passed he doubled his score. Zoey couldn't believe her eyes. She was the only person she knew that could play that good.

When Jacob finished the match he said how much fun it was, and got back to cleaning. Zoey asked Jacob how long he'd been playing game systems for. Jacob commented that that was the first one, and he'd never seen one until he got there. Zoey decided she wanted to see Jacob fail at something, and got one of Max's TV dinners. She cooked it up, and had Jacob try it. Jacob said how good it was, and ate the whole dinner. Zoey got a little frustrated, and grabbed one of Max's devils beers. Jacob drank it, and immediately got a buzz. Zoey tried a little of the beer and spat it out right away. Jacob laughed at her. Zoey made a face, and went to get Max's devils smoke, and his bong specifically for devils smoke. She packed a big bowl for Jacob, and gave him the bong.

Zoey said she would never condone a kid smoking and drinking but that he was a different case given his past. Jacob looked at it puzzled. Zoey huffed and told him how to use it. So Jacob did as she instructed, and ripped it, getting a huge hit champing it. Then Jacob breathed out and started to cough uncontrollable. Zoey quickly grabbed the bong from Jacob, and started to laugh at him. Then all at once Jacob stopped coughing, and his eyes turned solid black, and looked at the wall across from him. Zoey panicked and asked what he was staring at. He said everything. She asked what he meant by that. Jacob could only say that she had to try it, so Zoey took a small hit off the bong obtaining the same effect as Jacob.

When Zoey stopped coughing she stared straight ahead, and all she could think of was the meaning of life and the most intense emotional passionate feelings streamed through her. After a few seconds she started to get scared, and wanted it to stop. She couldn't move her body. They both sat there for 30 minutes before they could move again, however she still couldn't shake the feelings and thoughts from her mind. An hour later when she came down enough from the high. She went to her room, and grabbed her bag of weed and the other bong. She packed it, and took a hit. When she exhaled she felt herself calm down. She asked Jacob if he wanted to come down a little bit, but he grabbed the bong with the devils smoke in it and said no.

More impressed by Jacob than anything Zoey asked if he wanted one of Max's devils cigarettes. Jacob looked at her with wide black eyes, and said yes. Zoey felt creeped out by him, but got the cigarettes, and gave him one. Jacob lit the cigarette up and hit it. Zoey asked what it tasted like. He tried to give it to Zoey, but she said that she doesn't even smoke normal cigarettes. So Jacob did his best to described the cigarette to her. He said that it was like taking a huge breath of the cleanest air. Zoey pulled a cigarette out to try, when Max came in the door. Max stopped Zoey right away saying that one hit of the cigarette would kill her. Jacob looked at Max, and without even realizing it took another hit. Max was couldn't believe what he was seeing. He asked Zoey how many times he took a drag from the cigarette. Zoey said twice now, then Jacob took another hit, still not paying attention. Max told Jacob to stop, but Jacob said it was too amazing to stop.

Max looked at Zoey, and asked what else she gave him. Zoey told him that he tried everything, and liked all of it. Max just scratched his head in disbelief, and said whatever. Max sat next to Jacob, and looked at his eyes. He asked Zoey what happened to his eyes. She said it was a side effect of the devils smoke. Max could only shake his head grabbing the bong from Jacob, and torch the bowl. Later that night when everyone started to come down from their high. Jacob took the stinkiest poop. Zoey and Max decided to go out it was so bad. They told Jacob that he wasn't allowed to eat any more of the TV dinners, or the beer. Jacob could only laugh.

Whenever they took Jacob to the their favorite restaurant, which was the one that Zoey and Max went to on their first date, the people stared with disgust. Which made Jacob feel awkward, and he didn't much like going out. When people saw him they would call the cops, but the cops knew who was with Jacob, Max, and they didn't dare mess with him again. Which led to more crime, because of the lack of police activity towards Max. The criminals figured they could get away with stuff too. So things in their town got more hectic.

The three of them were on the news often. People from out of town would complain that the police weren't doing their jobs, and that they were afraid of a myth. The police would plead with them that they were telling the truth, and the only people who knew that they were telling the truth were the original town's people who stayed despite the growing gang activity. The people who did believe the police started to join Max as a following, which basically could be described as cross between a gang, cult, religion, and corporate organization. They often did charity work, and gave money to the poor. But they acted as a military group fighting other criminal organizations, and started privet wars where ever they deemed a priority. Max had no idea that all of the people that followed him were even doing these things in his name.

As the months passed Zoey and Max saw that Jacob was growing restless, only able to get out of the house when they did. They talked about what they could do to solve the issue, and decided that he could try going back to school. When they ran it by Jacob he was hesitant at first, but they convinced him that it would be fun, and he could have new friends. When Jacob gave in, the two of them went to the school to register Jacob. When they got there everyone knew what they were there for. The adults would talk amongst themselves, and say awful things about them, but Zoey and Max ignored the gossiping people, and walked strait for the registration table in the gym.

The woman at the table didn't notice them at first until Max cleared his throat. The woman jumped when she saw them, and stuttered asking how she could help them. Max said that they wanted to register Jacob for the coming school year. The woman apologized to them, and said that she thought it wouldn't be a good thing having a murderer in the school, and that it would cause outrage. Zoey said that every child has the right to an education, knowing she didn't care about that ideal. The woman insisted that he couldn't be allowed in to the school. Max asked if he could talk to the principle or someone of the status. The woman huffed, and went to get the principal. When the principal came to the table he was shock to see them, clearly not knowing that they were the reason the woman brought him there.

The man also stuttered like the woman, and asked what the problem was. Zoey said angrily that she demanded that Jacob be let in the school's curriculum. The man sided with the woman, and said that it wouldn't be a good idea. They went back and forth for 20 minutes before a man tapped Max on the shoulder. Max turned to see a half-blood smiling at him. Max greeted the half-blood, and the half-blood greeted Max back. The half-blood asked what the issue was. Max told him the trouble they were having trying to get Jacob into the school. The half-blood patted Max on the shoulder, and said to let him handle it.

Max grabbed Zoey by the arm, and pulled her away from the table. Zoey asked what he was doing. Max told her that a half-blood was going to take care of things. They waited for 10 minutes for the half-blood and principal to talk it out. Then the half-blood shook the principles hand, the principle didn't look pleased at all. The half-blood came to Zoey and Max with a smile on his face, and said that Jacob starts school next week. Zoey and Max smiled and thanked the half-blood. The half-blood said it was his pleasure, and left. Zoey took one last look at the disappointed principle, and the woman next to him, than they left. When they told Jacob the news, he didn't seem too enthused. Max and Zoey reassured him that he'll be fine, and said that he'll have a lot of fun. Jacob sighed and said ok. But the only thing Jacob could think about was the possibility of being abused again. So Jacob went to his room, and lay in his bed. He thought to himself "here we go again."

First day of school

Zoey was taking her sweet time getting ready. Max and Jacob were getting impatient, and Max told her to hurry up before Jacobs late for his first day of school. Zoey only said that beauty takes time to complete. Max would have drove Jacob himself, but he didn't have a car despite Zoey often offering him that she would buy him one. Max would refuse saying that he didn't want such an expensive gift. So it was up to Zoey to drive, but she had classes at 8:30 am, and Max wanted to be there for Jacobs first day of school. So Max couldn't just take the car. Once she was done and they piled in the car. Jacob again asked if he had to do this. Max and Zoey promised that he was going to have fun. Jacob fell silent, and waited for the car ride to be over.

When they reached the school, there were angry protesters from out of town everywhere. When the boy cotters saw the three pulling up they hoarding it, and started to beat on the car. Jacob got scared and begged them to take him home. Zoey said it was going to be ok, that this was expected. Jacob continued to beg them not to leave him. Max turned towards him, and put his hand on Jacobs's cheek and told him that it was going to be ok. Jacob asked what he did wrong, and if this was punishment, or if he was getting annoying. Jacob cried that he could change and be a better person for them. Zoey turned this time, and told Jacob to never think they don't like him. They just saw how anxious he was getting at the apartment the last few months, and thought this would be a good opportunity to get out of the apartment and find some friends while still being some what protected while out of their care.

Jacob shook his head, and said that he didn't want friends, that he was scared about people hurting him again. Max put his other hand on the other cheek, and said that he would protect him from anything that threatens him, and to not worry. Jacob calmed down a bit from hearing that, and said ok he'd do it. Max took a look at the people outside of the car, and said to Jacob "I'll go first." Max got out of the car, and the first person he saw he punched in the face sending him flying into the crowd of angery people. Max pulled out his gun and shot three times into the air above him. The people scattered, and a few cops walked up to him, and asked him not to cause a riot. Max asked the cops why they weren't doing their jobs, that Jacob is very scared. The cops apologized to Max, and started to clear the people away. Max opened the door for Jacob, and he got out. They walked together, Jacob in front of Max, to the entrance of the school.

News crews came up to them, and started asking them questions. Max told them to leave them alone, but they didn't. One of the reporters grabbed Jacob in attempt to stop him. Max grabbed the man's arm squeezing until it broke. The man fell to the ground and screamed. The other news crews decided to leave them alone. Once they were inside of the school, Max turned Jacob towards him, and said that everything will be ok. Jacob didn't feel the same way, and asked him one more time if he could just go home. Max hugged Jacob, and repeated that he'll be ok, and said to have fun. Jacob said ok and watched Max leave. As Max was leaving Jacob saw the angry mob through the glass windows of the doors, and he stopped Max calling out to him. Max asked if he was ok.

Jacob looked passed Max, then back to him, and asked if he would pick him up in this same spot. Max turned in the direction Jacob looked, and saw why he asked that. Max turned back to Jacob smiled, and said yes that he would. Jacob thanked him. Max walked back to Jacob and rubbed the top of his head, and turned to leave. Jacob watched him walk out of sight, then turned to see all the kids and faculty staring at him. Jacob sighed, looked at the ground, and walk in the direction he hoped his locker was in.

Jacob walked for 7 minutes looking for his locker. He turned a corner, and saw a group of kids talking. Jacob kept his gaze at the ground, and continued to walk. When he got closer one of the bigger kids said his name. Jacob looked up to see the big kid standing arm's length from him. Jacob shakily asked what he could do for him. The kid said that he was going to get his ass kicked for what he did. Jacob said he didn't want any trouble, and turned to leave. The big kid grabbed Jacob by the shoulder, twisted him around, and punched him on the cheek sending Jacob to the ground. Thoughts of his last school filled his head. Jacob grabbed his head with both hands, and started to shake it in an attempt to rid himself of the thought. Tears filled his eyes, and the big kid started to call him a pussy. The other kids started to laugh at Jacob, and joined in on the name calling saying that he was a murderer, a cry baby bitch, a pussy, a lame, amongst other things.

Jacob got up and tried to run, but the big kid grabbed Jacob by the collar of his shirt, and held up his fist to hit him again. Jacobs's eyes went hollow like they did in the past, and the only thing he could think of was it's the same thing no matter where I go. The big kid stopped for a second, and looked at how Jacob just accepted what was about to happen to him, and made the big kid feel uneasy. He shook the thought continuing his attempt to hit Jacob again, when a voice at the end of the hall stopped him. The big kid called out to the voices name as Alex, and asked what he was going to do about it, then noticed the group that Alex was with was that of 15 kids with him. The big kid dropped Jacob. Jacob fell to his knees, and sat on his heels unable to shake his thoughts. The big kid said whatever, and told the others in his group to come with him.

Alex and his group walked over, and stood next to Jacob, who was still sitting on his legs, arms lying limp in front of him. Alex knelt down, and put a hand on Jacobs shoulder, and asked if he was ok. Jacob didn't even know he was there until Alex pulled Jacobs head up by his chin. Jacob saw Alex and asked if he was going to hurt him too. Alex made a face with the expression of "really??," and said no. Jacob said good, and asked how he could help Alex. Alex interrupted Jacob, and asked why Jacob thinks he would hurt him. Jacob said that that's how all the kids treat him, and that he was worthless. Alex couldn't believe what he just heard, and asked why he would think that. Jacob said no just that's how he's used to people treating him.

Alex asked Jacob if he meant Max and Zoey treated him like that, or other people. Jacob said the boys and faculty at his last school. Alex asked if he was talking about his boarding school. Jacob said yes, and Alex asked what they would do to him. Jacob started to cry, and said that he wouldn't say, shaking his head. Alex placed his hands on Jacob's shoulders, and said it was ok, that he could tell him. Jacob looked at Alex a moment through tear covered eyes, and decided that he was trust worthy. So Jacob started to recount how the kids at the boarding school would treat him.

Alex asked why he didn't go to an adult about it. Jacob said that they didn't care and would often join in with the kids. Alex couldn't believe what he was hearing, and asked once more with emphases if there was anyone he could talk to there. Jacob just shook his head slowly. Alex looked at the other kids with him, and they all looked grim. Alex looked back at Jacob, and asked why he didn't call anyone like the police. Jacob said hollowly that they would never let him use the phone. Alex sighed, and asked why they treated him so poorly. Jacob snapped out of state of mind, looked at Alex seriously, and thought about the word that described him. Jacob thought if he told Alex what he was then he would treat him like the kids back at the boarding school would.

Jacob told Alex that he wouldn't say, and got up to leave thanking Alex for helping him. Alex grabbed Jacob by the shoulder to stop him. Jacob ripped his shoulder out of Alex's gripped turned towards him, and thanked him again for the help, but he couldn't tell him the reason why he was treated the way he was. Alex apologized, and said that none of his friends nor himself, would judge him. Jacob looked at Alex sternly, and Alex put his hand over his heart promising he would not make fun of him. Jacob grabbed both straps of his backpack hoping they would give him strength, closed his eyes, and said the word that's caused him so much pain, that he was gay.

When Jacob opened his eyes after no one said anything, looked around to see faces of sadness, faces of anger, faces pity, but the face that confused him was Alex's face which was a soft smile. Jacob asked Alex why he was smiling, and to not make fun of him. The other kids in the group looked at Alex, and started to smile and giggle. Jacob got angry, and turned to leave, but Alex stopped him. Jacob said that he was a liar, and he didn't want to talk to him. Alex seemed really shy to Jacob, when he said that he wasn't making fun of him. Then Alex asked if he could help him find his way around the school. The other kids giggled some more and dispersed. Jacob looked at the kids leaving, and how they were laughing. Jacob asked Alex still angry why they were laughing, and if it was directed towards him.

Alex smiled and ran a hand through his hair asking again if he could help Jacob find his way around. Jacob sighed not wanting too given to his confusion, but said yes to him knowing that there was no way he could find his locker and class before the bell rang. Alex excitedly said great, and asked Jacob what he was looking for. Jacob said that he couldn't find his locker. Alex asked for the paper listing his classes. Jacob got out the paper from in his pocket, and gave it to Alex. Alex took the paper and read it. After a few second of reading the paper, he said for Jacob to follow him.

As Jacob was following Alex through the halls, Jacob noticed all the people staring at him. It made Jacob feel uncomfortable. Alex saw how he was feeling, and said not to worry about them, that it would pass in time, and that they were just scared of him. Jacob said that he doesn't like that he scares people. Alex said that sense he did kill 7 people, and crippled a kid, then of course people would be afraid of him. Jacob stopped and said that he never meant to hurt anyone that he just broke under the pressure they were putting on him. Alex said that given the circumstances of his situation at the time, he said that he wasn't surprised he didn't do it sooner.

Then it hit Jacob, he stopped where he was, and put his hands on his head, and started to cry. Alex turned back and asked what was wrong. Jacob said that he couldn't believe what he did. That he couldn't believe he stooped so low as to kill and hurt other people. Alex said that he had no choice, it was do or die. Jacob said that there's never a good reason to kill someone, unless there is no other choice. Alex grabbed Jacob by the shoulders and said that there was no other choice to make, and started to recount how they treated him. Jacob just shook his head and said that they're dead now. That they are never coming back, and it's all his fault. That he wishes he was dead. Alex said not to let it get to him. Jacob looked at Alex and yelled "you didn't fucking kill them!!"

Alex took a step back, feeling the impact of Jacobs's sorrows, and couldn't think of a way to comfort Jacob. Then one of the kids watching them asked if all the stuff about how Jacob was treated was true. Jacob stopped crying looking around at the people in the hall listening to them, then back at the girl, and nodded. Everyone gasped, and a teacher walked up to them, and said that Jacob should come with him to see a counselor. Jacob wiped the tears from his eyes. Then he looked at Alex for his opinion. Alex nodded suggesting that he go. Jacob looked at the teacher and nodded. The teacher led the way, with Jacob following behind him. People stared at Jacob as they walked, but he didn't care keeping his eyes fixed on the back of the teacher's loafers. All Jacob could think about was how terrible of a person he was.

Once they reached the office, the teacher had Jacob sit down in one of the five chairs to the left of a door. The teacher told Jacob to wait there while he talks to the councilor. Jacob could only nod staring at the ground, tears still steady however calm he was now. The teacher put his hand on Jacobs head trying to give as much comfort as the law would allow, and then walked into the door next to him. About five minutes later the teacher came back out, and said for Jacob to go into the room. Jacob did as he was told. There was a jolly looking man who was half bold, and had a big white beard. The teacher introduced the man as Bruce. Bruce greeted Jacob, Jacob said Hello back. The teacher told Jacob to not hold back, and to tell Bruce everything. Jacob nodded, understanding the request. Then the teacher left.

Bruce started by asking why he never called the police about all the abuse. Jacob told him that they never let him near a phone. Bruce asked if they ever let him off the campus grounds. Jacob shook his head. Bruce stroked his beard, then asked for Jacob to tell him everything. Jacob was hesitant at first, but Bruce reassured him that it was in his best interest if he told him everything he could. Jacob still hesitated unsure of the consequences, but decided that Bruce was on his side. So Jacob told Bruce everything he could think of that happened to him, even how he felt up to when he first talked to Max. Bruce didn't say anything, only listened making upset faces when he heard the cringiest parts.

When Bruce was sure he was done he asked Jacob why they treated him like that. Jacob said the word he himself hated most, that he was gay. Bruce was leaning against his desk, then, suddenly got up and went to his phone. Jacob got worried and asked if he was in trouble. Bruce said that no, he wasn't, but he was calling to have an investigation started on the boarding school. Once Bruce was finished on the phone, he told Jacob that normally he'd have to get the police involved sense he talked about suicide, but given that he was under the protection of Max, and what that meant. He was instead going to call Max, and have him come to talk to Jacob. Jacob got worried that Max and Zoey would be upset with him and asked Bruce not to call Max. Bruce said that suicide is a very severe thing to talk about, and shouldn't be taken lightly.

Max was sitting at home watching adventure time, when his phone rang. When he answered it Bruce told him about how Jacob was feeling about what he did to the people when he was escaping the boarding school. Max panicked and said that he'd be there as soon as he could. When Max got off the phone with Bruce he called Zoey, and told her what he was told. Zoey panicked too, and said she was on her way to pick him up, but Max said that he was already out the door. Zoey said to meet him at a certain corner. Max acknowledge the corner and hung up the phone. Max ran as fast as he could worry filing his heart. He'd never been scared for anyone, other than Zoey. He'd always cared about Jacob, and to hear this kind of news made him hurt inside.

Max got to the corner before Zoey. Zoey pulled up with the window down and told Max to get in. They raced through the streets to the school. Zoey and Max went to the office, and asked were the councilor's office was located. The woman at the desk pointed at a door. Max knocked on the door, and Bruce said to come in. Jacob was still sitting in the same chair, but stood when he saw them. Jacob apologized to Max and Zoey for taking them away from what they were doing. Zoey walked up to Jacob and slapped him across the face. Jacob couldn't believe what she did, and stared at her shocked. Then Zoey held Jacob in her arms, and started to cry. Jacob held her back, and also started to cry.

Max asked Bruce what exactly happened. Bruce told him that one of the kids tried to justify what he did, and Jacob broke down. He continued to say that a teacher overheard what had happened to Jacob, and brought him here. Max turned towards Jacob and Zoey. He joined the hug, and said to Jacob that they love him, and that they couldn't live with themselves if he took his life. Jacob asked Max to repeat what he just said. Zoey said that they were a family, and that they loved him. Jacob pulled away from them, and looked at them oddly. Zoey asked why he was looking at them weird. Jacob said that he'd couldn't understand what they just said, and said how long it had been sense someone said that to him.

Zoey got closer to Jacob putting either hand on his cheek, and told him in a soft caring voice "I love you Jacob. You are a part of this family now, and I don't want to see any harm come to you" then kissed him on the forehead Jacob looked at Max, who repeated what Zoey just said, but a little different. Jacob got really light headed, and almost fell backwards, but Max caught him, and asked if he was ok. Jacob shook his head, and said that the only person that's ever said that to him was his sister. Max pulled Jacob up straight, and said that what they were saying was true. Jacob stood there for a second. Then, still in disbelief, said thanks that he loved them too. Jacob said that he'd like to go to class now. Max asked if he'd be ok for the rest of the day, or if he wanted to go home. Jacob just shook his head, and said that he was fine. Zoey and Max said ok, hugged him again, then let Jacob go to class. Zoey and Max stayed to talk to Bruce about different ways of possible therapy.

Jacob wander the halls looking for his class that he thought he was supposed to be in at the time, still bewildered and not able to grasp the full emotions he thought he was supposed to feel about what Max and Zoey said to him. As he was walking and contemplating, a teacher stopped him and asked where he was going. Jacob showed the teacher the paper with his classes on it. The teacher looked at it and said he'd take him to his next class. Jacob followed the teacher down the empty hallways to his class. Before Jacob went through the doors, the teacher stopped him, and said how sorry he was that he went through what he did. Before Jacob could ask the teacher how he knew, the teacher turned and left. Jacob watched he walk away before entering the class.

Everyone in the class stopped what they were doing, and looked at Jacob, even the teacher. Jacob felt uncomfortable, and handed the teacher his hall pass. The teacher didn't even look at it, and asked him to have a seat in any empty desk in the class room. Jacob chose a desk in the back corner of the room. He sat down, and pulled out the book for the class. As Jacob was opening it, the girl to the right of him asked if everything that people were saying about him were true. Jacob nodded, and everyone in the class room started whispering to each other, and Jacob noticed that everyone was paying attention to him. Jacob tried to ignore them, although it was hard. The teacher told everyone to quiet down, and the whispering stopped. The girl asked Jacob if it was true that it was because he was gay. Jacob cringed at the word, and slowly nodded. The class started to whisper again, and the teacher again told them to be quiet. The class continued as normal after that.

When the bell rang Jacob walked out of the class room, and was stopped by the girl that talked to him. She introduced herself as Elizabeth, and said that he should follow her. Before he could say no, she grabbed him by the arm, and pulled him down the hall. Jacob sighed and let it happen. She led him to a group of kids. They were all talking until they saw Jacob. Elizabeth introduced Jacob to a snobby looking girl named Lora. Lora asked why Elizabeth brought Jacob to her. Elizabeth told Lora that she thinks Jacob would be a good candidate for the gay alliance club. Lora said that there was no way she was going to allow a murderer into her club. Elizabeth tried to persuade Lora to let Jacob in the club, but she wouldn't budge. Alex walked up beside Jacob, and said it would make a sympathetic understanding for the club, then apologized to Jacob for suggesting to use him like that. Jacob acknowledges the apology.

Lora thought about it under those guidelines for a few seconds, then said yes, but Jacob refused the offer, and started to walk away. Alex stopped him, and said that it would be a great opportunity for him to find real friends who understand him. Jacob looked at him and said he didn't want to be a poster boy. Alex told Jacob that if anyone would understand him it would be in this club. Jacob thought about it sighed and said ok, that he'd do it. The other kids cheered except Lora. Jacob started to leave again, and again Alex stopped him, and asked if he could walk him to his next class. The other kids started to giggle. Jacob asked why the other kids would always laugh when he asked to take him somewhere. Alex blushed unsure of himself, and said he didn't know why. Jacob looked at Alex odd shook his head, and said yes to the request from Alex. Alex couldn't control his smile, when he asked for Jacobs's class paper. Jacob, frustrated by the mystery surrounding Alex, handed him the paper with his classes on it. Alex took the paper and read it, though he already remembered from earlier when he first read it, where Jacobs's next class was located.

As Alex started walking in the direction of Jacobs class, Jacob asks Alex if he's going to be late for his class. Alex says that he doesn't care. Jacob comments that Alex shouldn't be late for a stranger. Alex starts to blush again, and tells Jacob that he likes to help people. Jacob shakes his head and follows Alex down the hall to his next class. Alex tried to make small talk, and asked him about his family. Jacob sneered and said that his old family was dead. Alex kicked himself for saying that. Then he asked Jacob about Max. Jacob asked what he'd like to know. Alex asked if it was true Max had been shot several times. Jacob confirmed what Alex has heard. Alex commented how cool it was that Max was immortal.

Jacob ignored what Alex said and asked him if everyone at the school hated him. Alex said that everyone has started to understand what happened to him, and that he thinks they could like him. Jacob asked what that was supposed to mean. Alex said that it's a good thing considering the whole story. Alex said that he doesn't care about the deaths, but the word in the town was that of hatred for him, Zoey, and Max. Jacob looked at the ground and fell silent. Alex saw Jacob looked depressed, and asks Jacob how his first day is going. Right after Alex asked Jacob he realizes that he shouldn't have, because Jacob shakes his head and says that he doesn't want to talk about it. Feeling dumb, Alex apologizes to Jacob for asking the question in the first place. Jacob says its whatever, and to not worry about it.

Alex tells Jacob that he likes his white hair. Jacob says that it reminds him of his sister that passed away when he was a kid. Alex swears in his head, and again apologizes to Jacob. Jacob stops, and tells Alex that he doesn't know why he's so interested in him, but that he should just not ask any more questions. Alex apologizes again, and they walk in silence for the rest of the way to Jacob's class. When they reach Jacob's class, Jacob thanks Alex for showing him to his next class. Alex tells Jacob that he wasn't trying to make him feel upset. Jacob says to Alex that for whatever reason he's trying to talk to him, he's grateful for the company. Alex blushes, and says that it's no problem, that he's just trying to help the new kid find his way, knowing that he isn't there just to help Jacob find his way. Jacob thanks Alex for helping him, and walks into his class. Alex thinks to himself that he's going to figure out how to make Jacob understand why he's acting weird around him. Alex stares in the class room for a bit trying to see were Jacob sits, then leaves to go to his next class.

Jacob's class went about the same as the last class. People were curious about what happened to him, and said that he was brave but a terrible person for what he did. Jacob tried not to let the other kids discourage him despite how hard it was. when the lunch bell rang, Jacob walked to the lunch room by himself getting lost only once. When he walked through the doors to the cafeteria everyone stopped what they were doing fell silent, and stared at Jacob. Jacob was about to turn, and leave but Alex greeted him. Jacob shook his head, and asked Alex what he wanted. Alex said that he wanted him to sit with his group. Jacob said that he was just going to go to his next class, and wait for the bell to ring. Alex said to Jacob that he has to eat something. Jacob told Alex that he's used to not eating, especially when he's at school. Alex begs Jacob to eat something. Jacob looks at the room, and several people tell Jacob that he should eat something, including teachers. Jacob looks at Alex, and says fine.

Alex smiles, and says he'll stand in line with him for his food. Jacob tells Alex that he'd would rather just wait in line by himself. Alex's smile lessens, but says ok to Jacob. As Jacob was waiting in line, people would ask him the same questions he heard all day. Jacob politely said that he wasn't interested in telling his story for the rest of the day. The other kids were pretty understanding of Jacob's request, and left him alone. When Jacob got his food, he had a sense of relief when the woman serving him his food didn't spit in it. Jacob smiled at the woman, and thanked her. The woman smiled at Jacob for his politeness, and joked that it was her job.

Jacob did what Alex requested, and sat by him with his group, including Elizabeth. When Jacob sat next to Alex the other kids at the table greeted Jacob like he'd been their friend forever. Jacob wasn't sure how to react to the random friendship. Jacob greeted them back, and started to eat his none spat on food. Alex asked Jacob what he was doing after school. Jacob said that Zoey, Max, and him are going to a movie. Alex looked depressed and said ok. Jacob told Alex that he was free on Saturday if he really wanted to hangout. Alex livened up after hearing that, and said excitedly ok. Jacob didn't still couldn't figure out why Alex was so excited, and shook his head. The other kids knew what was going on between Jacob and Alex though, and laughed at Jacob's confusion and innocence.

Alex tried to make the other kids stop laughing, but Jacob asked before Alex could stop them, if he was only a joke to them. The other kids just smiled, and said to Jacob that they weren't laughing at Jacob. Alex made a cutting motion with his hand across his neck trying to make the other kids stop. The other kids laughed at Alex. Jacob shook his head, and stood up saying that he was done being there reason to laugh. Alex and the other kids told Jacob that they didn't mean anything by it, and pleaded to Jacob to stay. Jacob sighed and sat back down. Jacob told the other kids to not laugh at him anymore, that he's had the worst day, though not as bad as his past. The other kids said they'd stop laughing, and again said that they were not laughing at him to make fun of him. Jacob said ok and continued to eat.

There was a pause while everyone started to eat again, thinking of how to approach Jacob after what he said. Elizabeth broke the silence, and asked Jacob how he likes living with Zoey and Max. Jacob lit up and began telling the other kids all about his life with his new family. Which led to Jacob remembering what Zoey said about him being a part of their family. Jacob felt warm inside, and knew that he would never leave his new home.

The rest of the lunch was filled with small talk and laughter. When the bell rang for the next class, Jacob was actually sad that he couldn't talk to the other kids, and had to go to class. Alex asked if he could walk Jacob to his next class. Jacob said yes, but asked what his deal was, why he was so interested in him. Alex wanted to tell Jacob that he liked him, but he was too shy, and instead said that he was still just trying to help him out on his first day. Jacob looked at Alex weird and said whatever, and said that he could take him to his next class again.

As they walked through the halls Alex wanted to hold Jacob's hand, and motioned for it twice, and Jacob almost caught him twice. When they reached Jacob's class Alex asked if he had ever dated someone before. Jacob looked at Alex odd, and said that no he has never dated anyone. Alex smiled, and said cool, then left. Jacob was dumbfounded by how random Alex was, and stood in front of the class for a few seconds, before going into the class thinking how weird Alex was.

The rest of the day was good for Jacob. Jacobs classes were pretty boring, but the teachers and other kids were nice for the most part, understanding why he did what he did, though they all had the agreement that they didn't like that Jacob killed the 7 people that he did. Which Jacob could understand why. Alex would be waiting outside of Jacob's classes, asking if he could take Jacob to his next class. Jacob still thought Alex was sketchy, but aloud Alex to lead the way. When the final bell rang, Jacob couldn't wait to just go home and relax.

Alex asked Jacob if he could walk him home. Jacob told Alex that he was getting a ride from Zoey and Max. Alex asked excitedly if he could meat Max. Jacob said yea, that Max would be waiting for him at the front door. Alex followed Jacob to the front door to find Max waiting in the same spot he left Jacob that morning. Alex walked up to Max and held out his hand, and introduced himself to Max. Max looked at Alex awkwardly, and shook Alex's hand. Jacob walked past the two of them, and told Max that he just wanted to go home. Max sighed and told Alex that it was nice to meet him. Alex looked past Max and said goodbye to Jacob. Jacob just waved his hand, his back still turned to Alex. Alex looked a little sad that Jacob didn't seem interested. Max saw how depressed Alex was, and knew exactly what was going on. Max told Alex that Jacob's just new to the real world. Alex looked relieved to hear that from Max. Max said goodbye to Alex, and made his way to the door.

Max told Jacob that he would go out the door first. There were still a lot of people boycotting outside, though not as many. As they walked outside the people knew not to get to close for fear of Max. The news crews were braver however, and got close enough to ask Jacob if what they heard about how Jacob was treated at the boarding school was true. Jacob tried to ignore them and kept walking. The news crews kept pestering him. Zoey parked in the road right in front of the school blocking traffic, waving for the two of them to hurry up pointing at her watch, and mentioned when the movie was starting. Right before Jacob got in the car, a reporter, grabbed Jacob by the arm, and asked again if the rumors were true. Before Max could destroy the reporters face, Jacob yelled at the top of his lungs that all of it was true, and how awful he feels about hurting those people. Everyone in ear shot stopped as Jacob looked around at all the people, tears filling his eyes.

Max opened the car door and ushered for Jacob to get in. Jacob didn't get in right away taking a moment to get the courage to apologize for what he did. Jacob wasn't sure if people would believe him at this point, but he didn't care. He felt better about saying it however selfish it made him feel for just wanting the closer of openly saying it. Max placed his hand on the back of Jacob's head and leaned close saying "it's alright bud. They don't matter. Its the people that are directly involved in your life that are worth saying sorry to now. Other people just want you to feel as small as they can to make you feel like crap. But its over now and we're going to move into the future as best we can. You've spoken your peace, and there is no more need to feed the masses their daily dose of drama." Jacob sighed and slowly got into the car.

Once Max was in, Zoey started to drive away. As they were driving Zoey asked Jacob as he was wiping the tears from his eyes, how his first day went with obviously sarcasm trying to elevate the mood. Jacob laughed at her, and said that it was ok for what it's worth. Max asked if he'd still like to go to school. Jacob said he thinks it couldn't get much worse, and that he'd like to continue to go. Max and Zoey both said how wonderful it is that Jacob wants to continue to go, and how proud they were of him for facing his fears. Zoey says that they will go out for ice-cream, and after the movie to celebrate. Max asks Jacob if he wouldn't mind going to see a councilor about his past. Jacob said that he wouldn't mind. Max said great, and turned forward again. There was a pause in the conversation, and Jacob looked out the window and thought to himself "a real family, though."

ZOEY

OVER THE NEXT YEAR

As time passed everything started to look good for the three. Alex asked Jacob out, and they had their first kiss at a movie. Max and Zoey got married, and adopted Jacob. The new family was completely inseparable spending as much time with each other as they could. The people at Jacob's new school boycotting eventually stopped. Jacob's boarding school was fined, and many of the staff lost their jobs over the atrocities they did to Jacob. The kids at Jacob's school slowly excepted him, and found out how nice he really was. More and more people flooded into their town as news spread about Max, his genius wife, and murderous son.

Gangbangers were everywhere in the town doing as they please. And more followers of Max flowed into the town, trying to get a glimpse of him. News crews were haunting the three, and stayed outside their door only leaving when Max made them. All the excitement was starting to stress the three out. Zoey and Max eventually decided to move after she was done with collage at the end of the year. So as the school year was starting to come to a close, they got excited to move.

LAST DAY OF SCHOOL

Zoey was having the worst day of her life. She spilled red bull on her favorite lucky shoes, she miss spelled parquetry, and she was late for her last final. At the end of the day she exhausted, and just wanted get on her computer. As she was walking out the front door she saw Max and Jacob goofing around. Max was wearing his mask he made in limbo, courtesy of the half-bloods, which barley fit him as an adult. Jacob saw her first and waved to her. Just as Zoey was lifting her hand to wave back, the man from the apple bee's when her and Max went on their first date, shot her in the back twice. The man called out his gangs name and ran inside the school.

Many of Max's followers were present and chased after the man pulling out guns of their own. Zoey stood for a second, not believing what had just happened to her. Max and Jacob ran to her side. Max was fast enough to catch her before she hit the ground. Zoey was already passed out when Max caught her. Jacob started to cry as a circle of people formed around them. One man pulled out his phone and started recording what was going on. Max laid Zoey on the ground gently pulling the mask over his face to hide his anger from the people around him.

He hovered over Zoey as a rush of emotions and thoughts filled his head. He couldn't stop them from battering his mind, then everything went white, then black, then red formed in the middle of the blackness spreading outward. When he looked up people were either starring in awe, or running from him. Max felt bigger, stronger. His senses were more developed in a way that he knew what his body could do. He knew he wasn't his normal self. He looked at Zoey and flipped her on her back. He used his long tongue to get the bullets out of her back. Once he was satisfied he turned towards the doors he asked Jacob what he was. Jacob looked at Max with a little fear, and said he was a demon. Max looked back at Jacob a little surprised, but excepted it.

Max told Jacob to stay with Zoey. Jacob nodded, and Max ran for the doors. Max broke through the doors without stopping. The man taking the video on his phone followed Max. Max sniffed the air around him, and got the scent of the gangbanger. Max ran in the direction of the sent as fast as he could. Max noticed that he was on all fours like a dog as it felt more comfortable. His hands, however, still looked like hands.

So he figured he must still have the same shape as a human. He noticed the sensation of wings on his back, though, he knew they didn't feel like they had any feathers or a membrane to be able to fly. He felt bigger too, he figured 8 feet tall, standing. His skin looked like it was burnt to a crisp, and was flaking bad. His tongue was as he realized was long, maybe two feet.

As he raced down the halls he looked back to the man following him still taking the video. Max called out to the man to keep up. Max wanted the world to see what he was, so they'd leave his family alone after. Max finally made it to a hallway with two of Max's followers were standing on the edge of a wall leading to another hallway, pistols drawn. As Max approached them, they looked terrified, but the fear quickly went away as they realized that it was Max expecting nothing less from him. Max didn't even stop to talk to them, and turned into the hallway. Max saw the gangbanger hiding behind a desk to one side of the hallway. The hallway was a dead end, and Max knew the gangbanger wasn't getting away.

The gangbanger stood up fear gripping his throat as he started shooting at Max, but the bullets would just hit Max and fall of his body. Max grabbed the man by his torso digging his fingers into the guys body. The man screamed in pain. Then Max used his other hand to grab the man's head, and pulled it off his body like a cork on a bottle. Max tossed the man's head to one side, and dug his tongue into the body through the neck. Max pulled out a glowing white orb which was the man's soul, and ate it. Not thoughts but sensations, feelings, emotions, the smell of familiarity, filled Max's mind. Max looked back at the three men watching the horror, then sniffed the air.

Once Max caught the scent of another gangbanger the previous gangbanger knew, Max jumped through the window at the end of the hall landing on a car in the parking lot next to the building. Max sniffed again, and ran in the direction of the smell. People he ran past screamed running from him. Max didn't even care though, he was on a mission. Max found a house were the smell of the gangbanger he was looking for was coming from, and plunged through the door taking everyone in the house by surprise. The gangbangers in the house had no idea how to react before picking up guns and to start shooting at Max. Max immediately got to work killing all of them. One gangbanger got away and ran out of the house. Max ran after him, and pinned him to the ground. The guy bagged for his life as Max ripped the man's head off, and ate his soul getting all the information he needed to find a new batch of gangbangers.

Max ran through the town killing as many gangbangers as he could find. Max's followers were up in arms also fighting the gangbangers, trying to help him. the cops had no idea where to begin, and called for the national guard. The national guard also didn't know how to quell the situation. The civilians started to leave the town as quick as they could. It was about 10:00 pm when Max came to a house with the last gangbangers he knew about. The cops and national guard were posted up two blocks down the road. Max's followers were behind cars in front of the house in a fire fight with the gangbangers.

Max ran in front of the house, and ordered for the shooting to stop on both sides. When the shooting came to an end, Max ordered the gangbangers to come out of the house. The gangbangers knew they didn't have a choice, and slowly made their way out of the house. When they were all out Max offered them a deal. Max told them they could stay in the town and die, or they could leave the town and never come back. The gangbangers didn't hesitate in replying that they would leave. Max told them to start walking in the direction where cops and national guard were the two blocks up the road. When the group reached the lawman Max told the cops that the gangbangers were to be escorted out of the city, and his followers would be pardoned. The cops and national guard could only say yes.

As they cops led the gangbangers away Max went back to his followers. Max grew back into his original form, his mask, now the diameter car tire, fell to the ground. Max noted that the mask must have grown with his body. A young man that was one of the followers greeted Max, and

Max greeted him back. Max thanked them for helping. They all were grateful to have help. The young man handed Max a Wal-Mart bag with clothes and a hoodie in it. Max looked at his death suit, and saw how torn up it was from stretching. Max took the bag and thanked the man. The young man asked how he turned into the demon. As Max was changing he told the young man that he had no idea how he did it. That it just happened without his control.

When Max was finished dressing himself he asked the man if he could drive him to the hospital. The young man looked at Max with a smile. Max asked why he was smiling. The young man said that Zoey was fine, and that he would take him. The young man led Max to his car. As Max got in the car he thought to himself "what if I only ate one of the seeds??"

A PLAN FOR RETRIBUTION

Zoey woke up feeling drowsy. As she sat up in bed she saw Max and Jacob watching family guy. Zoey laughed at them, and the two turned to see her. Jacob got up from his chair and hugged Zoey. Max got up from his chair and gave Zoey a kiss. When they were done greeting each other Zoey asked what happened. Max said that a gangbanger shot her in the back. Zoey looked surprised and asked how she was alive. Jacob said wide eyed that Max turned into a demon. Zoey showed as much surprise as she could. Zoey asked how it happened. Jacob told her that Max glowed white and grew angel wings, then he caught on fire and transformed into a demon with a long tail, and the feathers burned off of the wings. Zoey asked again how it happened. Max said that he felt a rush of emotions for what happened to her, and what he wanted to do to the gangbanger, then it happened.

Zoey asked Max if he killed the gangbanger in that form. Jacob interrupted saying "yea and all the rest of the gangbangers in the town."

Max asked Zoey if it changed their relationship. Zoey said "it didn't before, so why would it now." Max blushed and thanked Zoey, kissing her again. Jacob got out his phone, and pulled up the videos of Max, showing Zoey. Zoey couldn't believe her eyes. Then Zoey saw Max eating a soul, and asks what it was. Max told her it was a soul. Zoey asked why he ate it. Max said that he doesn't remember much, but he remembered that he ate it for food. Jacob asked Max what it tasted like. Max said it was like eating a devils delight TV dinner. Zoey asked if he got anything else from the soul. Max said that no it was only sustenance. Zoey put her hand under her chin and thought for a moment. Jacob noted that it couldn't be a good thing, and Max and him both laughed.

Zoey asked Max if she could conduct a series of tests on his body. Max said sure. Zoey asked next what happened to her after Max chased the man. Jacob said that he stayed with her all the way to the hospital. Jacob continued to say that Max took the bullets out of her back with his tongue, and greenish white foam was coming out of the bullet holes. Zoey asked what the doctors said about it. Jacob said that her wounds would heal in a couple of days, and how strange it was, that all they needed to give her was a saline drip. Zoey got more and more intrigued by the events that transpired the day before.

Zoey again put her hand under her chin, and thought. Max and Jacob looked at each other nervously, and asked what was up with her. Zoey thought for a minute longer before saying that she had a plan. Max asked "a plan for what??"

Zoey looked at Max as seriously as she has ever looked in the past, and said "were going to end the greed, corruption, poverty, hunger, and every other complication in America, and we'll do it together." Max started to smile, enlightened by the idea of vigilantism. Jacob said that he didn't want to hurt anyone. Zoey said that he didn't have to. Jacob let out a sigh of relief, and sat back in his chair. Max asked what her plan was. Zoey told him "first we'll move to Colorado. Then I'll begin testing your abilities, and how your body functions with just your soul. Then once I've developed enough tech to build you a proper suit of armor, modern armor of course, we'll start ridding this world of the evils that plague it."

Max said that he was already happy to help her. Then Max remembered that he has an army also, and told her about the people that helped him yesterday. Zoey could only smile at how randomly fate worked to their advantage. Jacob and Max looked at each other and again said that she was stating to scare them. Zoey said that they'll move tomorrow. Jacob instantly objected to the idea, noting his relationship with Alex. Zoey agreed that it wouldn't be right to part the two so far away from each other, and thought about it for a minute, then said to Jacob that if his family allows it, Alex could stay the summer at their place. Jacob got his phone out and called Alex, knowing how serious Zoey was right at the moment. Jacob walked out of the room to pitch the idea to Alex.

Max asked why she wanted to move to Colorado. Zoey said two things "it's rural, and weed is legal." Max laughed, and shook his head. Max got just as serious as Zoey now, and asked what her plan was to take back America from all the corruption. Zoey said, "first we take out as many slave operations as we can, stealing all the money from those putrid men. Then when we have the off the book funds needed, we go after the drug lords. After that we get evidence from the corrupt corporations and banks and file a lawsuit against them. And lastly we fund a campaigning president that we agree will bring the country into a good or better place than it already is, so he or she gets the position. And after everything is done and over with we give the money back to the people."

Max asked how she could find all these people. Zoey simply said, "The internet, they're not that sly. People are easy to catch on the web you just have to find the right places to look." Max smiled and said that he loved her. Zoey smiled back and thanked him for the help that she has always wanted what's best for the world, and now she has the possibility in her grasp. Jacob was still on the phone when he walked back in the room, and said that his family would let him stay one month out of the year and spring break, but they wouldn't have the money to fly him out. Zoey said that she would pay for him. Jacob got really excited and walked back out of the room. Just as Jacob was leaving, on the TV peter griffin started one of his epic fights with the giant chicken. Max and

Zoey watched it, and started to laugh. Zoey said to Max "we could do it. We could change the world."

Max turned to Zoey and said "together we can…. Let's play batman for real."

THE WAR ON CORRUPTION

It was 10:00 pm and Max was punching a drug dealer in the stomach with the claws attached to his suit of armor constructed by Zoey sending the man flying in agony. It was the fifteenth drug house he and his followers, now called the Raxel, raided this week alone. Zoey asked through the intercom in Max's helmet how the raid was going. Max told her that another 30 minutes and they'd be done. The family, Max, Zoey, and Jacob, have been in their war against the corrupted America for two years. They found success in every fire fight they engaged in. they bought a large house in Colorado like they wanted, in the middle of nowhere, making sure to get the runes carved on the door frames including the massive door in the ground close to the house for a mech Zoey made that linked to the house through the basement.

Zoey did outrages tests on Max gathering unbelievable information on the soul, and during the two years she constructed a mech that could focus and amplify her own soul into energy forming a temporary sword or a shield out of the palm of the left hand that lasted for about 10 minutes of continues use then it would have to recharge for two minute unless the shield was taking considerable damage. She also built an unmanned robot she could pilot from the house so she could help in the raids, but she would never take a life. Zoey made more tech for Americas military, cops, and the Raxel. The Raxel made a tent city around the house, and started training for their fight against the corruption. More and more people came to them wanting to help.

America no longer feared Max, and cheered when they saw him in public often asking for autographs. Zoey would help the cops find the gangs, murderers, drug dealers, thieves, rapist, slave merchants, and corrupt business man. the cops would storm their places of business, and arrest what Max wouldn't destroy. The progress was slow to start until the good people recognized their sacrifices, and they got the help they needed. Max never liked what he had to do, but he didn't care too much about it knowing that the people he was killing were just scum.

They brought criminals from as high as illegal business from banks, to pedophiles on the internet, to simple car thief's, whether it was justice by their hand or Americas lawmen. Criminals were starting to flee America, but most of them were caught by Zoey's information she found on her computer, driven by many long nights of red bull and hard work.

Jacob would stay at the house being home schooled by Zoey. Alex would visit him for the month of July, and they'd have a huge fourth of July party with all the people living around their house. The party turned into a festival of sorts, and people from all over the world would come and share their culture. Max was so happy that people from every nation could collaborate with peace and harmony. Max thought to himself that life would be perfect if everyone could come together like they do at their fourth of July party. Max believed he could change the minds of people for the better if they felt safe enough to talk to each other without hate in their hearts.

Zoey asked if Max would be home that night through the mike in his helmet. Max told Zoey that he had one more raid in three days, then he'd be home for two weeks. Jacob said how excited he was to see him, and Zoey told Jacob not to interrupt, but Zoey did comment on how Jacob has been talking about him for the last two and have weeks sense he has been gone on missions that Zoey had him carry out. Max said that he couldn't wait to see his family, and told them he loved them.

As Max punched a man in the temple, he asked how things were going at the UN. Zoey told him that they were still hounding the American ambassador to make her and him help their countries too. Max told her that they should talk to them in a few weeks. Zoey agreed and noted how heated the debates were getting. Max asked Zoey if the American ambassador told the other countries that it wasn't his choice to make them do anything. That they were free agents. Zoey said that she keeps telling the ambassador that, but he only gets the same responses from the other countries. Zoey tells Max thinking more about the severity of the situation at the UN, that they should probably go to the UN as soon as he gets back.

Max ran at a man shooting an assault rifle at him, grabbed it from the man and used the weapon to strike the man across the face knocking the man to the ground, and tells Zoey that he agrees with her. Zoey says she'll make a phone call to the American ambassador tomorrow. Max tells her ok, and then says that he loves her. Zoey tells him that she loves him too. Jacob yells in the background that he loves Max also, and Zoey yells at him who makes Jacob and Max both laugh. Zoey smiles at them to herself. Then the communication ends, and Max is left to his work.

THE BREATH OF WAR

It was 2:00 pm when Zoey and Max stood in front the UN ambassadors. Max was the first to say how wonderful it was to finally talk to all of them. The French ambassador told Max that he demands that he help their country with its problems, and the rest of the countries ambassadors start to yell the same thing. Zoey tells them all to shut the Hell up. When everyone quieted down, Zoey tolls them that they were not there to be ordered like dogs to do their bidding. The room went into another up roar, saying that they could demand whatever they wanted from people like them, and that they were monsters with no importance. Max yelled into the microphone on the podium in front of them to calm down. The room got quiet again, and Max told them again that they are not pieces of meat. Then Max tries to explain that it was their intent to help the rest of the world, but they were still so overwhelmed with their own country at the moment, and they'd get to their countries as fast as they could.

The entire room glared at them. The Russian ambassador tells the two that that's not good enough, and they want them to help now. That it was their fault they were getting all of Americas criminals. Zoey tells him that they are only two people, and can only do so much. The English ambassador told them they must not care about the rest of the world, and that the two of them were being greedy squandering their talents only on America's problems. Zoey was about to tell the English ambassador to go screw herself, but Max stopped her and asked why they don't believe them. The Russian ambassador told the two that they should build them the same technology for them like Zoey did for the Americans. Zoey told the Russian ambassador smugly not if he asks like that. The Russian ambassador stood up from his chair and asked if they wanted war. All the ambassadors stood up and started to agree with the Russian ambassador saying that it was a good idea, that America has been hording their accomplishments sense world war two.

Max tried to calm them down, but was unsuccessful, so he slammed his fist into the podium shattering it into pieces. Everyone went quiet, and Max told them that they don't belong to America. That they don't need to hate America for something that Americans have no control over. The German ambassador yelled out bull shit at the top of his lungs, and called Max a liar. The German ambassador went on to say that Max was a product of American engineering. Max was shocked at how blind they all were. Then the American ambassador walked up next to the two, and told the people in the room that it was true, and America held no power over Max and Zoey as they have been doing all this on their own will. The room called the American ambassador a liar as well.

The three, Zoey, Max, and the American ambassador, were dumbfounded by what was going on, and couldn't think of how to make them understand. Then it happened. Spain was the first to say they were going to war against America, then Russia, England, France, china, India, japan, and then the rest of the room all said it. Insults started flying at the three, as the room started to clear out. The three stood there waiting for the last person to leave.

When it was just them in the room, Zoey talk first, and said that they would help the Americans with whatever they needed. Max agreed with her. The ambassador thanked them, and said he doesn't know what to do. Zoey told him to get to the president and immediately start prepping for war. The man threw up, and Max asked if he was ok. The man said no, and started to cry. Max started to rub his back telling him to be strong. Zoey told Max that she was a little scared herself. Max said as long as he lives the rest of the world will not take America. The ambassador wiped his mouth and thanked Max and Zoey for their help and dedication. Max told the man not to thank them yet, that it's going to be a long road, and many people are going to die. Zoey commented on how stupid this war is going to be. Max says to her "its war…"

THE JAVELINS' WORD

Jacobs sitting in the massive room that houses Zoey's mech underneath the house doing work on the soldiers on the east side of what's left of Americas boarders with Zoey's robot she made years ago for raiding drug lords compounds. Zoey walks past and says good morning to him. Jacob replies good morning. She asks him what its looking like on the east side. Jacob tells her that it's still the same. It was 12 years into the war, and America was losing bad. Zoey's technology was the only thing keeping America alive. Though, the other countries had their own technology, massive unmanned mechs of their own.

It was 10 years into the war when America surrendered, and the nations didn't care. The other countries wanted to destroy what was left of America to keep it from coming back. The other countries got greedy and wanted everything they could get their hands on. When American soldiers surrendered they would be executed on the spot. The civilians on the other side of the front line were killed or enslaved. America was scared for its life, and everyone young and old fought for their freedom. The president was killed 6 years into the war, and what was left of the government formed a council to make decisions. America is on its last leg fighting as hard as it could to save itself.

Jacob and Zoey stayed in the house in Colorado in enemy territory, because it was the only place she could work on and make repairs to her mech. The enemy found the house in the 4th year of the war, and have

103

been dropping bombs, rockets, missals, and anything else that explodes on their home trying to destroy it, but the runes carved on the house kept the house from even getting dirty. When Zoey had to leave for more supplies, or to fight the enemy, she would have to hold the left hand of her mech up with her shield activated as the doors leading outside from the room housing the mech opened to keep the inside from being blasted. Max was on what was on the east side of America fighting with the American soldiers and what was left of the Raxel. Jacob used the unmanned robot Zoey built to fight next to Max side.

Things were tense, and Zoey couldn't stop thinking about all of it as she told Jacob that she was going out to find and destroy the rockets that keep hitting the house. Jacob told her to be careful, that the enemy mechs were getting higher in number around their area. Zoey thanked him for the information, and made her way into her mech. Zoey powered her mech up, and activated the comlink to talk to Jacob and Max. She asked Max how his day was going. Max replied through the helmet of the same suit of armor he used in the drug raids, that he was doing ok but the man he just killed wasn't as happy. Zoey laughed a little bit, and thought how awful war has twisted her mind.

Jacob couldn't even look at himself in the mirror anymore the more he killed other people. Zoey stood her mech up, and made it grab a massive pistol, assault rifle, and the metal backpack that carried extra battery packs for her mech and ammo for her weapons. She raises the left hand of the mech and activates the energy shield focused by her own soul, and opens the huge door above her leading outside. Right as the doors open explosions start going of all around the area. Zoey makes her mech jump up above the doors, and quickly pushes the button in her mech that closes the door. Once the door is closed and Jacob and the inside of the house are safe she dashes in the direction she thinks the closest rocket might be with her shield still activated above the mechs head.

Once she clears some distance from the house the explosions stop, and she slows her mech to a walking pays. The night before Zoey mapped out where she thinks the rockets hitting the house were coming from, and continues to head in the direction she thinks the closest one is. When she finds it there are fifty other enemy unmanned mechs guarding the rocket silo. Zoey starts dashing at the first mech, and uses her mechs energy sword to cut the mech in two. The other mechs react to the attack, and start shooting at her, but Zoey's mech has the advantage of speed and the ability to be nimble. It doesn't take her long to dispatch the enemy mechs, and lets the rest of the soldiers on the ground not in mechs to leave before placing charges on the silo destroying it. Zoey moves from silo to silo with the same results.

Jacob and Max would check in on her constantly making sure she was ok. It was 1:37 pm and she had just taken out the 29th silo, and was moving to the next one when she came into a wide opening with scorched dirt for about a mile in diameter. Zoey tells Jacob and Max about how odd the circle was. Max asked what could possibly do that much damage. Jacob asked if it could have been a huge bomb. Zoey dug her mechs hand into the soil, and said no, that the area was too perfectly symmetrical for it to have been a bomb, and none of the surrounding trees were blown back. As she examines the dirt she notices how deep the dirt is scorched. Zoey gasps, and said she knows what it is. Max fearing the worst asks what it could be. Zoey whispers "the javelin"

Jacob and Max couldn't believe what they heard. Jacob tries reasher himself by telling Zoey that the javelin is a myth, knowing that she's probably right. Max tells Zoey to get out of there. Zoey agrees and stands her mech up to find that she's surrounded by thousands of unmanned enemy mechs. Zoey smiles, and tells Jacob and Max that she's not getting away this time. Jacob asks what she's talking about. Zoey tells them the situation. Max yells at her to run as fast as she can. Zoey shakes her head knowing that there was no way out. She tells them that she has to fight, and makes her mech dash at the closest enemy mech. Max tells her she can't fight them all. Zoey tells him she doesn't have a choice, that there are too many of them for her to just get away. Jacob tells Zoey to just stay alive. Zoey could only smile at the challenge.

Zoey fights for two hours, and her mech has taken a lot of damage, but not enough that she is worried. She's felt relived that she can still get away, but was angry at how many repairs she'd have to make. Then a yellow light shines down on her. Zoey swears and raises her mechs left hand activating its shield. A pink light shoots down from the sky decimating everything in the area. Max asks her what's going on. Zoey tells them that it is the javelin. Jacob and Max both tell her to leave, but there are still too many mechs to get away. When the pink light stops, Zoey's mech has lost its right arm, but is still able to fight. Zoey immediately pulls out her mechs pistol, and attacks the closest mech trying to make a brake for it. But there are still too many of them for her to get away. Then the yellow light shines down again making Zoey drop the pistol and lifts her mechs hand again activating its shield. When the pink light strikes her mech again it brings the mech to one knee. When the pink light leaves her, her mech is barely able to stand, but she continues to fight the other mechs with the energy sword.

Zoey tells Max and Jacob calmly that she's going to die in the next blast. Max, holding a man by the throat, stops what he's doing and holds the man in the air. Jacob stops shooting his robots weapon. They are both in disbelief. Max starts telling her that he loves her. Jacob starts to cry, and tells her "please don't die."

Zoey tells them as the yellow light rains down on her again "I-I love you guys. My life would have been plain and uninteresting without you..." Zoey lifts her mechs left hand one more time trying to activating what's left its shield. Zoey lets a tear stream down her cheek and as she smiles and starts to say "I love y-" then nothing.

MAX

PEACE IN LESS THAN A DAY

Jacob turned in his chair and started to cry, cursing the war. Max just stood in the middle of the battle field holding the soldier by the throat unable to move. White light filled his sight, then darkness. Instead of red filling in his vision, it was yellow that brought him into focus. Max blinked a few times. He wasn't angry anymore. He was just tiered of the violence, tiered of the hate in the world. Max dropped the man letting him fall to the ground. Max knew what he was this time, an angel, or close to it. He felt as though he was back in limbo as a kid again. The armor had broken free of his body in the transformation leaving him in only the black suit he ware under his armor.

Everyone on the battle field stopped what they were doing, and stared awe struck at what Max was. Max looked at one of the enemy soldiers and flew over to him. Max asked the man if he spoke English. The man could only nod. Max grabbed the man, and took flight. The man screamed, not knowing what Max was going to do. Max told the man to calm down, that he wasn't going to hurt him. The man did calm down a little, and asked what Max was going to do with him. Max asked for the man's name. The man said his name was Nicholas. Nicholas asked again what Max was going to do with him. Max told Nicholas that he was going to end the war, and he needed a translator. Nicholas laughed at Max saying that the war will never end.

Max thought back at what Zoey said once, "we're fighting to save humanity from itself, and nothing, not even death, will stop us." Max told the man that he will end it today no matter the cost. Nicholas said that Max wasn't even an angel, that angels have white wings, and he had black wings. Nicholas said that no one would take a boy with black wings seriously. Max asked were his closest camp was. Nicholas said he'd never tell him were his allies' camps were located. Max let go of Nicholas. Nicholas screamed as he plunged to the ground. Max flew next to Nicholas as he fell, and asked him again were the camps were. Nicholas told Max there was one just south of where they were. Max grabbed Nicholas again, and flew south.

Max flew for 15 minutes before the first camp came into view. Max flew down into the middle of the camp, setting Nicholas down. Nicholas fell to his knees, and grabbed a fist full of dirt saying something in his native language. Everyone in eye sight of Max stopped what they were doing and pulled their weapons on him. Max picked Nicholas up from the ground and told him to ask for the person in charge of the camp. Nicholas told Max to screw off, and made a dash for a group of soldiers telling the soldiers to fire at Max. Everyone started to shoot at Max. Max immediately got frustrated holding out his hand and formed a transparent yellow bubble grow around him deflecting all the bullets. When the soldiers realized they were just wasting ammo they stopped firing.

Max let his shield down, and yelled to Nicholas to ask for the person in charge. Nicholas refused Max again. Max told Nicholas that he can take out the entire camp if he wanted to. That he just wants to talk to the leader. Before Nicholas could answer several gunner trucks pulled up, and pointed their turrets at Max. Soldiers got out of the trucks, and aimed their weapons at Max. A man swearing in French asked what Max wanted. Nicholas told the Frenchmen to get out of there, that Max was there for him. Max looked at Nicholas yelling, and figured out what he was saying by the way the Frenchmen turned and fled for the truck. Max dashed faster than the eye can blink, and grabbed the Frenchmen by the caller of his shirt.

Every soldier in the area ran up on Max weapons pointed at him. Max asked Nicholas to translate for him. Nicholas nervously said yes realizing he had no choice, pushing his way through the crowd. When Nicholas was ready, Max told the Frenchmen that he is to tell the countries to call of the war. The Frenchmen laughed so hard at Max he started to tear up. Max slammed the Frenchmen into the closest truck, which was only a few feet away. The soldiers were ready to fire, but the Frenchmen waved his hand still laughing. Then the Frenchmen said through wet eyes, why would he take one freaks threat seriously. Max told the man he will destroy the entire camp if he doesn't comply. The Frenchmen held out his arms, palms up, and said in English "try it."

Max let go of the Frenchmen, and walked to Nicholas grabbing him by the fore arm. Max pulled Nicholas in the middle of the clearing, and told him not to move from this spot until he comes back for him. Nicholas started to laugh until he saw into Max's eyes. Nicholas grew scared, and nodded accepting Max's mercy. Max flew into the air so the whole camp was visible. He held out his hands facing the camp letting yellow orbs of energy form in either palm. He held the orbs for a second knowing what he was about to do, and let beams of yellow energy shoot from the orbs streaking them across the camp causing massive explosions. Max destroyed most of the camp before flying down to Nicholas.

Nicholas was crying at all the devastation around him. Max held out his hand, and asked Nicholas where the next camp was located. Nicholas said he wouldn't tell him. Max told Nicholas that if he doesn't come with him, that he was going to destroy every camp on the east coast until the war was ended but he could help end it by telling the person in command of the next camp what lays in wait for them. Nichols looked at the ground, and grabbed Max's hand. Max held Nicholas by the fore arm, and took flight.

It was another hour before the next camp came into view. Max landed in the middle of the camp letting go of Nicholas. Nicholas didn't waste time, and immediately asked for the commanding officer. People were acting the same as the last camp with their weapons pointed at Max, and very skittish. There was only one soldier that understood and could talk to Nicholas, and asked Nicholas if he was in any danger. Nicholas said it was a matter of life and death for the camp. When the translator for Nicholas told the other soldiers, people in the area froze and looked at each other. The man talking to Nicholas said that he'll get the commander right away, and ran for a communication device.

They waited for 8 minutes, before five gunner trucks pulled up. The commander stepped out of one of the trucks, and walked up to Max without fear and asked what he wanted, that he was in the middle of a meal. Nicholas waved for his translator to come over. The translator ran next to the three. Nicholas told the soldier to translate help what he was going to say for the two, Max and the commander. The man agreed to the request.

Max said to the commander that he was to tell the countries attacking to retreat, and sign a peace treaty with America. The commander looked at Max for a few seconds and turned to leave. Max grabbed the commander by the arm, but the commander pulled it away and continued to walk. Max left his hand in the air making a fist. Max didn't want to do it again, and told Nicholas to tell the commander what he did to the last camp. Nicholas quickly described to the commander what Max is capable of. The commander said bull shit in his native tongue, and got into his truck. Nicholas started to yell to everyone in every language he knew to run. The soldiers that understood him just looked at each other, and told Nicholas to take Max and leave before they throw them in the brig.

Nicholas's translator started to walk away, but Max grabbed the young man by the arm, and told Nicholas to tell the young man to stay with him. Nicholas did, and the young soldier asked what was going to happen, with a little sarcasm. Max flew into the air. Nicholas begged the young soldier to stay with him the young man asked why he was so afraid. Nicholas told the young man that everything he said about Max was true. The man started to look at Nicholas sideways with a smile. Nicholas told the young man that Max gave mercy to him, and stay close with him. Just as the young man was about to tell Nicholas off, beams started to rain down on the camp blowing everything up. The young man jumped and ran next to Nicholas. As the devastation was going on around them, Nicholas and the young man started to cry at the loss of life. Bodies were everywhere around the two when Max landed next to them.

The young man dropped his weapon, and held out his hands begging for Max not to kill him. Max put the man's hands down, and said, Nicholas translating for him, that he was not going to kill him, because he was to be the witness of the devastation. Max also said for the young man to tell the other camps to cease fire. The young man wiped the tears from his eyes, and ran for a communication device. Max held out his arm for Nicholas to grab. Nicholas shook his head, and said that he didn't want to be a part of it anymore. Max told Nicholas that he was the only person that's experienced both incidents, and that he is the one that can save the other soldiers from the same fate. Nicholas put a hand over his face shaking his head, and grabbed Max by the fore arm. Max flew once more.

Max went to six more camps with the same result. On the seventh camp the word got around about Max. It was 9:34 PM when the allied countries fighting America started to retreat back to their countries. Within two weeks the countries were completely out of America. A peace treaty was signed after the soldiers were out of the country. Max was present for the treaty, still in his second form as an angel. Max during the treaty demanded that the other countries repair everything destroyed in America, and all the people enslaved be brought back to America. One of the leaders of America also demanded that the other countries give a considerable amount of money for the suffering of America. The other countries started to argue that fixing America's buildings was enough, but Max threatened them, and the countries grudgingly agreed to the demand. When the countries were done with singing the peace treaty, now one shook hands.

Max flew back to his house in Colorado. When he came into view of the house the ground was black for a hundred yards in every direction, massive ditches everywhere. The house itself was fine. Max landed on in front of the door, changing back into his normal self. Max opened the door, and called out for Jacob as he walked into the house. Jacob didn't answer. Max looked around the house for a little bit before finding him in the basement. Max walking down the stairs into the massive empty room, and saw Jacob was using the equipment that maneuvered the robot he used during the war. Max called out to Jacob. Jacob looked up surprised to see Max. Jacob said hey to Max, and continued what he was doing. Max asked why he was using the robot. Jacob said that there was a lot of crime going on in the area of the robot, so he decided to help the local law enforcement.

Max got close to Jacob, and patted him on the back of the shoulder. Jacob stopped what he was doing and turned to Max saying "I miss her."

Max replied "if there was any way she wanted to go this would have been it… I'm lost though. I don't know what to do. I loved her so much."

Jacob told Max "she was a beast about it." They both laughed hurting more that they couldn't cry, though, she wouldn't have wanted them too, and they knew it.

Jacobs last words

62 years passed, and America was not doing so well even after the other countries helped repair their home. America struggled to rebuild their crops, industry, and bring peace to their torn lives. Max went out to many countries on missions to save the enslaved Americans from the war not brought back. Even though the countries gave back the money they took from America, there was still issues with trading with the countries. There was a lot of hate in the planet, and the only thing keeping more war away was Max. Max and Jacob did fulfill their obligation to the other countries, and helped them with their problems in order, crime and such, which led to a little less tension, though, it was

still there. Max, Jacob, and the entire country of America, mourned for Zoey when they put an empty coffin in the ground outside of Jacob and Max's house in Colorado. Thousands of people showed up for the service. Max and Jacob fell into a depression over their loss for 3 years.

It was when Jacob got married to Alex that they got out of their depression, and found happiness in life again. As Jacob got older, Max stayed the same age, which made him feel awkward around Jacob. Jacob didn't mind though, and still treated Max as his dad. The older Jacob got the more Max worried for him. Max knew Jacobs life was coming to an end, and when Jacob ended up in the hospital obvious he wasn't leaving Max grew sad. Max knew what was coming... loneliness.

Jacob coughed into his hand as Max reached for Jacobs cup of crushed ice. Alex was sitting next to Jacob on his left, and Max was sitting on the right. Jacob took a drink through the straw, and gulped hard. Alex was holding Jacobs hand, and reassuring him that he was going to be ok. Jacob laughed at the idea that he was going to live. Jacob told the two that he was going to die soon, that his age hit him earlier that day, and nothing was going to save him. Jacob started to close his eyes when Max gave Jacob a slight jolt back to life by calling his name. Jacob asked Max if he did it right, if his life was worth it, if it was worth taking so many lives.

Alex answers before Max could telling him that his life has been one struggle after another, and he should be proud of his accomplishments. Alex reminds Jacob of all the good he did in the name of peace and salvation for all the innocent people he saved. Making a hard choice that leads into a better outcome. Saving as many lives as he could. Making choices that no person should have to do in their life time. Alex tells Jacob that he made the right choice his entire life, and shouldn't be ashamed of who and what he was. Jacob asked if he was going to Hell for all he's done in his life.

Max looked grim, and said yes, that god doesn't look highly on murder at all for a good reason or not. Max then says that if he asks for forgiveness god might let him into heaven. Max then says that that's what the bible says, and he wasn't sure if it was true or not. Jacob pauses for a second then says "I can't ask for forgiveness, because the things I did had to be done, and nobody else would take the first step to do it. No, I except my punishment in the afterlife. It's what I deserve…"

Max asks Jacob if he is scared. Jacob laughs and replies that if Hells anything like what Max says it is, then no he is not scared. They pause for a few minutes, then Jacob's vision starts to go black, and with his dying words says to both Max and Alex "I love you…" Jacob closes his eyes, and the heart monitor flat lines. Alex jumps up to get the doctor, but Max stops him. Alex asks what he's is doing. Max points at Jacob, and tells Alex that he's already excepted death, and to bring him back would hurt that. Alex looked at Jacob for a second, and nodded sitting down tears filling his eyes. Max unplugs the heart monitor, and sits back in his chair.

Ten minutes pass when the nurse walked into the room with Jacob's medicine. The nurse goes for the doctor also, but Max stops her as well. The nurse having respect for Max and Jacob tells Max that she still has to get the doctor, but she'll tell the doctor not to attempt to revive Jacob. Max thanks the nurse knowing that it was past the time of helping him anyways. The nurse calmly leaves to find the doctor. Max gets up and pulls out a devils cigarette putting it in his mouth. Max leans over Jacob's peaceful body, and puts a hand on the side of Jacobs face, and says "I love you too Jacob…" and leaves to smoke his cigarette.

THE FIRST LORD

Max spent just as much money on Jacob's funeral as he did on Zoey's, and just as many people came. In the end the entire world knew that Jacob was a good person. That's all Max wanted for Jacob was for people to love him as much as Zoey and him. Max berried Jacob next to Zoey. After the funeral, Max walked through the empty house completely lost. The question ran through his head again "what do I do now??"

Days passed, then weeks. Max gave most of Zoey's technology to America, but only the stuff he didn't think would hurt the world. Many people came to his door asking for help, but he couldn't bring himself out of the house. He asked the half-bloods that frequented the house how Zoey and Jacob were doing. They told Max that Zoey was doing great in heaven, but was sad that she wasn't with him, and was sad that Jacob had passed. They said that Jacob got Max's cottage in limbo thanks to Tanner and Darren, and that he was doing fine and content with his duties with Thimblest.

Max was happy that Zoey and Jacob were doing fine, but he still didn't have a goal other than finding a way back into the afterlife. Max asked the half-bloods on earth if they could smuggle him into the other plain, but they said that they could only transfer small things like food and items. Max asked them if there was another way to get into heaven or Hell, but the half- bloods said that there wasn't.

Max couldn't believe what the half-bloods, and started to go on expeditions to holy places searching for a doorway into the afterlife. Years passed, and Max couldn't find anything. Not even suggesting that there was a doorway into heaven or Hell. Six years passed before Max went back to his home in Colorado in defeat. It was just as empty as when he first left it, filled with only memories and dusty furniture. Max woke one day after weeks of not sleeping, and walked outside. He fell to his knees and looked at his hands. Anger swelled inside of him. He thought "what's the point of all this??" he looked up at the sky rage in his eyes, and yelled out "why am I here??" he waited for an answer.

When none came to him his heart broke, and his mind snapped. Darkness filled his eyes, then red. When his vision came into focus he stood up. Max was tall now, he guessed he was over 50 stories tall. Max walked over to a nearby lake and looked into it. He saw a wolfs head on a harry body with demon wings. The skin on the tip of his snout had receded half way back leaving only bone. Max stepped back, and couldn't understand the world anymore. All he could think about was finding a way to see his family again. He had it in his mind that if he dug under every holy site and ancient place on the planet, one of them would have a doorway back into heaven or Hell. So he took flight towards Middle East.

The world was terrified of Max and attacked him with everything they had, jets, mechs, tanks, artillery, etc., but Max was not trying to hurt anyone showing no interest in bothering with any mortals. He started with the dome of the rock, and found nothing. So he went to the another holy site, and found nothing. he moved from one spot to the next, destroying everything he deemed a holy or ancient spot of significance digging to find this doorway he was even sure didn't existed. Max went at it for weeks without stopping. Once he tore through the middle east unsatisfied, he turned his focus towards Europe and their ancient sites.

One day when Max was walking towards Greece, he was confronted by five mechs similar to Zoey's. Confused and blinded by his emotions, Max ran to hug one of them thinking it was Zoey here to save him from his misery. Scarred by Max's sheer size, the five pilots of the mechs opened fire on the advancing monster. Max couldn't believe what was happening to him. Max quickly defeated the mechs, and tore open the cock pits to find strangers. Max grew into a deeper depression when he set the pilots of the mechs on the ground leaving them alone in the wilderness, but alive and let out a howl.

God had been watching Max sense he was put on earth, and grew more and more worrisome by Max's knowledge of the power that's been given to him via the seeds. God calls Lucifer at his house asking if he wanted to make a deal to take out Max. Lucifer laughs at God at how Max has gotten out of control. God makes a deal with Lucifer that if he defeats Max he will take his house arrest off, and give free rain over earth for the next 1,000 years. Lucifer agrees that he could use a little exercise after being stuck in the house for so long. He tells god that he'll do it, and excitedly makes his way to the door in the basement in his house. Lucifer waits by the door until the ankle bracelet clicks and falls to the floor. Lucifer smiles and opens the door. In the room is a white swirling vortex of energy in the ground. Lucifer doesn't hesitate, and jumps into the vortex.

Max was just outside of Athens when the ground shook beneath his feet. Then a crack ripped across the ground opening up. Lucifer puts a hand on the edge of the crack lifting himself up to be in full view for everyone to see. Lucifer was a little bigger then Max and instead of a wolf he had a goats head with massive horns. Max quickly asks who the new beast was. Lucifer replied with his name. The people watching TV thanks to the news reporters in the helicopters overhead were terrified, and didn't know what was going to happen. Whether they were going to join forces or fight. Max quickly changed from sad to excited, and asked Lucifer if he was going to take him back to the afterlife.

Lucifer laughed at Max, and told him that he was there to kill Max on the orders of God's words, and in return God gave him freedom to do what he wants to the planet for 1,000 years. Max was stupefied by the idea of God giving the world to Lucifer. Max let out a defining howl, and told Lucifer that he'll will never give earth to him. Lucifer laughed even harder, and asked if Max was challenging him. Max growled and told Lucifer so long as he lives no harm will ever come to earth. Lucifer snarled, and said to Max that he shouldn't talk that way to a angel. Max laughed at Lucifer, and called him a bitch.

Lucifer broke at the insult, and rushed Max. Max was ready though and dodged Lucifer's punch. Max through a punch of his own, and clipped Lucifer under the jaw. Lucifer retaliated and struck Max in the side of the face. Max staggered, and punched Lucifer in the stomach as quick as he could getting two hits in. Lucifer put his hands together and brought them down on Max's back, Max wrapped his arms around Lucifer to keep himself from going to the ground. Lucifer continued to hit Max the same way five times before Max lifted Lucifer up and slammed him on his back. Max sat on Lucifer's body and started to strike Lucifer in the face as fast and as hard as he could. Lucifer grabbed one of Max's fists with one hand, and Max's throat with the other. Max was still punching

Lucifer as Lucifer got to his feet still holding Max by the throat. Lucifer tightened his grip on Max's throat, and tossed Max, then took to the air.

Max got up as quick as he could, and chased after Lucifer. Lucifer leads Max to Athens, and stopped still in the air above Athens. Max looked around at where he was. Max asked Lucifer if he would leave the people the area out of this, and he would he follow him wherever. Lucifer told Max that he would destroy every city to make him fight. Max thought about all the lives that were going to be destroyed in this fight, and snapped losing control of himself. Max roared which made Lucifer smile. Max was filled with rage, that he still had to fight people to maintain peace on this planet.

Max held up his hand, and like when he was an angel, a beam of energy, red this time, shot from the palm of Max's hand showering Lucifer. Lucifer was taken by surprise, and was hit directly by the blast. A huge explosion erupted. The people in the city screamed out in horror. Many of the people were already trying to evacuate the city. When the blast cleared Lucifer's arms and chest were bloodied with black blood. Lucifer was in a state of rage too now. Lucifer told Max a few of his plans for what he was going to do to the planet. Max was already enraged and nothing Lucifer said was going to make Max any madder. Max sent another shot of energy at Lucifer but Lucifer sent his own beam of black energy at Max. the two beams connected and an even greater explosion the size of an atom bomb rang out into the sky. They both met in the middle of the explosion, and started throwing punches at each other.

They fought for 24 minutes in the sky before Lucifer wrapped his arms around Max, and flew to the ground slamming Max into a building. Lucifer laughed as Max was slow to get up. Max wiped the blood from his mouth, and charged Lucifer. They stood in one place punching ceaselessly without blocking or dodging waiting for one another to give ground. It was about two hours later when they both were getting exhausted. They paused for a moment to catch their breath leaning against a building. People were still trying to get clear of the city as the armies started to move in to attempt to control the situatio.

More and more mechs appeared resembling Zoey's mech. As they cautiously moved into position Lucifer laughed and pointed them out. Max quickly yelled at them to leave. Lucifer noted Max's concern, and stood up. Lucifer laughed as he walked towards the mechs. Max told Lucifer to stop. Lucifer laughed again, and started running at the mechs. Max chased after him. The pilots in the mechs opened fire on Lucifer, which did nothing. Lucifer grabbed the first mech closest to him and punched it in the stomach killing the pilot. Lucifer tossed the mech to one side, and moved towards the next mech. As Lucifer reached for the mech Max grabbed Lucifer's arm with one hand, and punched Lucifer with the other. Lucifer grunted and punched Max back, and continued to attack the next mech. The pilot of the mech throw his gun away knowing that it wasn't doing anything, and pulled out the massive knife. Max was still punching Lucifer when the pilot of the mech attempted to stab Lucifer, but the blade wouldn't puncture Lucifer's skin.

Lucifer looked angrily at the mech, and grabbed it by the head. Max started to punch Lucifer in the face to try and distract him. Lucifer tried to shove Max away, but Max was persistent and wouldn't quite. The pilot of the mech started to punch Lucifer too, which seemed to work a little. The pilot of the mech told the other pilots to start using melee attacks. The other mech pilots through down their weapons and joined in the brawl. Lucifer was over whelmed by all the punches, though only Max's seemed to do the most damage. Most of the time the pilots of the mechs would just try and hold Lucifer's arms and legs to open him up for Max. this went on for several hours before the last mech was put out of commission, and it was just Lucifer and Max again throwing punches.

Exhausted again, they stopped and leaned against buildings. Lucifer told Max that he was going to kill and eat every human on this planet. Max was breathing hard, and it was hard for him to talk. Lucifer made fun of Max asking if a demon child had his tongue. Max simply said to Lucifer he was never going to take control of earth. Max lifted hand grabbing Lucifer's face, and with everything he had left shot one last beam of energy at Lucifer's face. Lucifer wasn't prepared for it and took the whole blast to the face killing him, and destroying many buildings around Lucifer. The only thing that was left of Lucifer was his body as it slumped to the ground.

Max walked over to the body, and shoved his hand into the corps pulling out Lucifer's sole. Max held the ball of energy in his hand for several minutes before eating it, and giving him energy to at least walk again. Max slowly walked away from the corps that started to disintegrate into black goop. Max walked for the rest of the night back to where Lucifer sprang from the ground. Once Max found it he started to dig. He dug for hours trying to give himself hope that this was the only way to get back into Hell. Max dug and dug, and didn't stop until things started to get hot, and turn into molten rock. Once he hit the molten rock he started to swim and search for a portal. Max looked for a week, and came up empty handed. So Max turned back into his original form, and curled into a ball covering his face with his hands wishing he could cry.

1,000 YEARS OF THOUGHTS

Max had been drifting in the thick liquid rock for 1,000 years now contemplating how to get back to the afterlife. He's learned to control his powers, and turn into any of the three forms he previously changed into. He found how to be in his original form with wings. But he still longed to be with Zoey and Jacob. Max thinks of every possible way to get back to the other plain and see his family, but nothing comes to mind. He starts to hate God and Lucifer for what they did to him. Granted they made it so he found Zoey and Jacob, but now he couldn't see them. It drove him mad that he was left with no purpose to his new life.

Then his head came into contact with a metal sphere no bigger than a basketball. Max grabbed the sphere, and noticed how light it was, even for him. Max tried to bend and mold the metal sphere by hand, but the metal was too strong. Max thought about what metal would be too hard for him to form, and decided he should ask someone about it. Max knew however that no human would know how to help him. So he thought about the half-bloods. Then he thought about what Lucifer said about God sending him after him, and figured no half-blood angel would ever help him. Max then thought about his fight with Lucifer and what the half-blood demons might say to him. Max thought that maybe the half-blood demons would treat him as their ruler…. Maybe. But it was the only chance Max had. So Max turned into his third form, grabbed the sphere, and made his way out of the hole. It took Max several hours to find the hole again, and he started to re-dig after the time that eroded the earth almost completely back to normal.

While Max was in seclusion from the outside world, many things changed. The structures of the cities were elegant and breath taking. There was world at peace, and everybody was happy and content. The hole that Max dug was now a tourist attraction where people took selfies. No one really believed the stories anymore, after there was a burning of all the records of Max and the things he did, to keep the world sane. So on this particularly beautiful summer day with the birds chirping and a nice cool breeze, people were not prepared to see Max's hand in third form grab the edge of the hole. People stopped what they were doing and stared at the massive hand. Then Max's head peeked out of the hole, and people took a step back unable to believe what was happening. When Max was fully out of the hole, he changed back into his original form, the form of his human body. People started taking videos and photos of Max.

Max shook the stares off and took a few steps forward sprouting black angel wings, but before he could take off a man stopped him. Max asked how he could be of help to the man. The man asked Max if he remembered who he was. Max shook his head. The man told Max to remember the party at God's mansion. Max thought back and tried to remember the people he met that night, but couldn't place a name to the face again shaking his head. The man sneered at Max, and told Max that he was Jesus. Max got very excited, and asked Jesus if he was there to take him to heaven. Jesus told Max that he has been labeled a rogue soul, and was to be eliminated. Max couldn't believe that God still wanted to kill him, but then again he offered Lucifer the world in exchange for killing him.

Max tried to explain to Jesus that he wasn't a threat to anyone, and that he just wanted to see his family again. Jesus told Max that Zoey was imprisoned. Max got into Jesus's face and asked what for. Jesus told Max that she was trying to make other soles agree that he was a good person. Max cursed and told Jesus to tell God that he should let Zoey go. Jesus told Max that she would never be set free. Max through down the metal ball, and told Jesus that if he wins the fight against him that Zoey is to be let go. Jesus laughed, and told Max that they would fight in three days, but it wouldn't save Zoey. Max asked where they were going to fight. Jesus told Max that he would find him. Jesus then turned and walked away.

Max was furious when he picked the sphere up. People around him had no idea what was going on, and were baffled. Max shook his head and took flight. It took most of the day to get back to his house in Colorado. When Max arrived there were several half-blood demons already waiting for him. Max landed and greeted the half-bloods. The half-bloods greeted him back. Max asked how he could help them. One of the half-bloods spoke for the rest of them, and started by thanking Max for freeing the demons from Lucifer's evil rain. When they were freed they came to realize that they never really like Lucifer or torturing souls. They told Max that they were able to make Hell a great place to live, though there was still punishment for being a bad person on earths plain in the form of a prison sentence. Max said how grateful he was for helping them, and asked how Jacob was doing. The half-blood told Max that Jacob was doing very well and still lived in his old cottage working for Thimblest.

One of the half-bloods asked Max if that was the heart of the planet, referring to the metal ball in Max's arms. Max looked at the sphere and asked if that is what its was called. The half-blood told Max that it's a very rare metal, and it can only be found in this plain in the center of planets. Max asked what it could be used for. The half-blood said that it could be used for anything. Max looked at the half-blood and asked if it could be made into a sword. The half-bloods looked at each other awkwardly then back at Max, and asked what he was going to use the sword for. Max told the half-bloods that Jesus wanted to fight him.

The half-bloods looked nervously at each other, and talked amongst themselves. They said to each other how they owed it to Max for freeing them from Lucifer, and how it would more than likely start a war. They talked about it for half an hour, before they asked Max when he was supposed to fight Jesus. Max told them three days. The half-bloods talked for another 16 minutes before agreeing to help Max, but they asked for a favor. Max told them anything. The half-bloods asked if they could use his house for a headquarters. Max agreed to the request, and moved to open the door. Before Max opened the door a half-blood asked Max if he knew what would happen if he killed someone with a sword like the one he's going to get. Max admitted that he had no clue. The half-blood told Max that if he kills someone with the sword their whole existence would be erased, their body, their sole, everything would be put back into a life force. Max looked at the half-blood and asked if it would kill God. The half-bloods went pale, and only one of them nodded. Max said nothing and opened the door.

THE SECOND LORD

The next two days were filled with activity. The half-blood demons built a forge to mold the heart of the planets into what the half-blood demons called a divine sword, able to destroy both the body and soul. The half-blood demons also trained Max how to use a sword. Max caught on pretty quick though he had to slow his movements for the half-bloods. The half-bloods new that by making this sword that they would more than likely starting a war with heaven, and was using Max's house as one of their base of operations. Max agreed to let the half-bloods use the house even after the event that he should die. Max told the half-bloods it was a thank you gift for making the sword, and putting their lives in danger.

The half-bloods warned Hell what was about to happen, and they also started to prepare for the inevitable fight. Hell was not pleased to hear what the half-bloods did on earths plain, though they knew they would have done the same. Max asked the half-bloods if they would move Jacob to middle of Hell. The half-bloods told Max that they were already evacuating limbo as a precaution. Max was pleased to hear that, and thanked them.

The news found out about the fight, and aired it over the TV. People had actually forgotten about Max's house, and there was a search to find Max's house. All the people that found what they believed was Max's house camped out around it. Only about a hundred people actually found Max's house and pitched tents, which made Max feel uncomfortable. He didn't want to make a spectacle of the fight, and it didn't take long for Max to want the fight to be over with. This, Max thought, was not the way he wanted to return to his home in Colorado. He honestly had hoped that the people of earth had thought of him as a hero for taking out Lucifer, but now he felt like he was made to be the bad guy. Max thought back to what all he and his family had done for earth.

On third day Jesus walked in the middle of the circle that formed out of the spectators his own divine sword in hand, and waited for Max. The half-bloods took the precaution of waited in the basement so that hopefully heaven wouldn't see that they had taken part in helping Max. Max opened the front door, and everyone that made up the circle started to whisper to each other about the legends of Max, and made room for the two men to duke it out. Jesus called out to Max and mentioned that he was impressed that Max even got out of the house. Max told Jesus that he didn't want to fight him, that this was all a big misunderstanding. Jesus laughed and asked why he was begging for his life. Max tells Jesus that he just wants to see Zoey and Jacob again, and that they don't have to fight. Jesus yells to Max to stop wasting time drawing his sword.

Max shakes his head, and walks toward Jesus drawing his own sword. Max takes a stance four feet away from Jesus. Jesus smiles as Max asks him again if they could stop fighting. Jesus shakes his head and tells Max that the only way someone is walking away is if the one of them dies. Max sighs, and says "fine, let it be done," and Jesus leaped towards Max, but Max parried Jesus attack. Jesus throws strike after strike only hitting air and metal. Max is quicker and stronger then Jesus, and Max knew it.

For the next 22 minutes Max tried his best to convince Jesus to stop fighting, and showed Jesus how much quicker he was then him. But Jesus wouldn't listen, and grew more and more determined. Jesus was getting tiered. Max saw this and when he blocked the next attack he grabbed Jesus's sword hand and yelled to Jesus to stop fighting. Jesus told Max that he would never stop until he was dead. Max asked why he was so determined to continue. Jesus told Max it's what he had to do, or die trying. Max looked Jesus straight in the eyes, and new exactly what he meant understanding his own determination. Jesus noted the look on Max's face, and said "then you do understand… I'm sorry brother." Jesus pulled his sword away from Max and lunged at him, and Max let Jesus sword graze his cheek while driving his sword into Jesus stomach.

Jesus fell to his knees dropping his sword on the ground. Max helped Jesus lay on his back. Jesus smiles at Max and says that he knew Max was never the bad guy. Max wanted to cry. He only talked to Jesus briefly at the dinner party in heaven, and never would have expected him to be so noble, though it was Jesus. Max says how sorry he is to Jesus, but Jesus doesn't care about it, and says he was glad to have met Max as a servant and now as a warrior.

Yellow energy started to flow from the middle of Jesus chest into the shape of a tree then disintegrate. His body started to disintegrate into the energy tree until nothing was left. The people that made up the circle were crying, though nobody called Max anything bad knowing that Max tried the entire time to stop the fight. Max picked up Jesus's sword, and stuck it in the ground next to where Zoey and Jacob were buried. Max thought about what it would be like to fight God now that it was inevitable, and how much more powerful he would be in comparison to Lucifer and Jesus. Max thought about the other planets hearts, and the possibility to make armor. Max turned into his third form and made for the heavens saying "come and get me God"

New armor

Max went to different planets in the solar system looking for more heart of the planets. He flew to mars, Jupiter, and Saturn. Each metal was a different size based on the size of the planet, Jupiter being the biggest, about the size of and SUV wheel. Max decided that that would be enough for making armor, and flew back to earth. Upon arrival of his home, there were soldiers outside of the house. Max landed in front of the group still in his third form. The soldiers panicked and aimed their weapons at Max, but didn't fire. Max turned back into his original form setting the hearts down, as he did a soldier came up to him. Max greeted the man, which through the man off guard at how polite Max was. The solider greeted Max back, and shakily told Max that he was under arrest. Max smirked at the man and asked how he planed on arresting him.

The soldier said he was just going to have his men start shooting if he didn't comply. Max told the soldier that it wouldn't work, that normal weapons wouldn't hurt him. The soldier tried to plead with Max not to hurt anyone. Max told the soldier that he never wanted to hurt anyone, that it's always been about being with his family in the other plain. The soldier said that he destroyed the planet and killed thousands of people last time he was around. Max asked where he heard that from. The soldier told Max that that's what the legends were about him. Max couldn't believe what he was hearing, and admitted to the soldier that he only destroyed ancient places, and never hurt anyone. The soldier looked dumb founded.

Max sighed and started to tell the soldier what happened from the time he was first brought back to earth to the present. The soldiers huddled around him and listened in awe as Max told them his story of heroism and loss. The soldiers asked questions often. It took Max more than an hour to tell most of his story, and his reasoning for why he was fighting.

The soldiers asked what happens now. Max told the soldiers that there will more than likely be a war between heaven and Hell, and it will take place on earth also. The soldier then asked if there was anything they could do, and Max told them to just stay out of it. The soldiers understood what was going to happen, and confirmed Max's request. Max thanked the soldier for understanding and believing him. As the soldiers were leaving, one of them asked if he was going to fight God. Max looked at the solider and said that he hoped so. The soldier got an awful taste in his mouth and walked away.

Max took the heart of the planets in the house one at a time. The half-bloods were in a frantic state running around the house. A half-blood greeted Max, and Max greeted him back. Max asked what was going on. The half-blood told Max that heaven did find out about them helping Max, and the war already started, and it wasn't going well for them. Max apologized for asking for their help and putting them in this situation. The half-blood said that it was their choice, and that it was probably going to happen anyways after Lucifer was defeated. The half-blood inquired about the heart of the planets in Max's arms. Max asked the half-blood if the metal could be used to make armor and a shield. The half-blood said that yeah it could be made into the gear he requested, and stopped two younger half-bloods.

The half-blood told the two younger half-bloods to take the metal to the blacksmith that was still set up in the basement. The younger half-bloods took two of the hearts and made their way down to the basement followed by Max who carried the last heart. The same half-blood that made Max's sword was still there crafting other stuff. The blacksmith greeted Max and Max greeted him back. The blacksmith asked what all the metal was for, and Max told him what he would like made out of the metal. The blacksmith told Max that it would take six days to complete the order, and that he need to get some measurements first. Max agreed and let the blacksmith take what he needed, and over the next six days Max trained more with a shield this time.

Max didn't sleep the entire six days, and often asked how the war was doing in Hell. Most of the half-bloods would just shake their head, others would say simply not good, and the rest would tell Max the whole low down, that specific territories were taken, and how many human soles and demons were killed or captured. The more Max listened to the news the more Max worried about Jacob. Max grew more and more resentful towards God. Max wouldn't let God get away with killing Jacob.

When the armor was finished Max put it on, and held the shield. The armor and shield were so light that it felt like he was wearing street clothes. Max also thought the armor looked pretty epic. The blacksmith half-blood showed Max where there were two slits in the back of the armor were Max could sprout wings if need be. Max thanked and complemented the blacksmith for the work. The half-blood said that it was no problem, and that it was his pleasure. Max trained in the armor for two days before three half-bloods ran to Max looking panicked. Max told the three to calm down and tell him what the issue was. Only one spoke, and told Max that the news caught God at the Patriots football stadium. Max shook his head and smiled. The half-bloods looked odd at him. Max said "it could have been any other team, but he chose the Patriots." The half-bloods snickered at each other.

Max sighed and made for the door. All the half-bloods stopped what they were doing and wished Max good luck. Max thanked them, and walked out the door, and told them that if he dies that there will be nothing to protect them. They told Max that they were already prepared for the situation. Max waited at the front door for a few minutes then grew his black wings and left the house for the last time to face God and unanswered questions.

THE THIRD LORD

Max flew at an even pass so that he wouldn't get warn out. Thoughts flowed freely through his head. He thought about how this never should have happened. Max didn't dwell on the fact that he could be erased from existence. He thought more about where he was at in limbo, and how content he was despite being killed every day, but it was a life he could live with he knew his punishment was just. He also had people that were counting on him too. He didn't understand the point of any of this, and now he was put in the fate of the universe. Max just wanted it to be over at any cost.

When the stadium came into view Max closed his eyes to calm himself down and focused his mind. He'd learned to do it when he was floating in the center of earth. It was snowing, and Max couldn't help but think of how beautiful it was. Max saw before he landed that there were seven angels with God, and God himself was wearing some epic armor too. Everyone in the stadium was quiet, and waiting for them to talk. Max spoke first and yelled "what was the point of all this, why am I here??"

God said to Max "you were meant to help people, but you only sought to destroy. You are unstable and need to be dealt with."

Max, "I'm not unstable. I admit there were a few times I snapped, but I never hurt anyone innocent."

God, "you killed so many people, and destroyed so many meaningful structures. What do you have to say for it??"

Max "I'm sorry, but the situation arose and I did my best to control the situation as best as I could. Why don't you understand that??"

God "you were sent here to fix the universe. Why did you not understand that??"

Max "because you never fucking told me."

God "watch your tongue child."

Max "or what you'll kill me. You're already going to try"

God laughs and says "you cocky child, the 8 of us are more than enough for you."

Max yells "then bring it on dad," pulling out his sword taking a stance.

God smiles and signals for the 7 angels to attack. The angels smirk confidently and rush Max. Max ran at them and swung down on the first angel bringing her to her knees while blocking another angel with his shield. There was a loud ring as the metal connected and wind rush from the force of the blow. The angles were strong but Max was still stronger and faster. Max knew it would be an easy fight, and it didn't take long for Max to take out two of the angels with ease. They, the remaining six fought for 10 minutes before Max brought it to an end. Max wasn't even breathing hard when he took his stance again and waited for God to make his move.

God sneered as he lifted his massive hammer with ease. Max sprouted wings and charged god in the air. God lifted his hammer stopping Max's sword making the entire ground shake, and the loudest noise and gust that the football fans had to shield their ears. God was able to stop the blow though it was enough to bring him slightly off balance. Max brought his shield around and stuck god in the side of his helmet. God punched Max in the chest sending him flying into the other end of the stadium. God levitated and chased after Max, but Max was ready for him, and charged back. They connected weapons again making another defining ting.

They swung again and again at each other only to hit a shield or the handle of a hammer. God was stronger but Max was quicker. Every time they connect the force would push the people in the bleachers off their seats making most of them leave. News crews were filming the whole fight, and the world was in an uproar. It was an hour into the fight when it took to the air. They fought back and forth sending each other flying into buildings and through the air until they crashed into the ground and started to fight. Every time Max would land a blow God was able to move his bodies armor into the path of his sword which his sword wouldn't even penetrate god's armor. It started to frustrate Max. There were only a few spots from what Max could tell where he could get his sword past the armor, but god knew it and kept Max from capitalizing on it.

They fought for 9 hours on the ground until they took to the air again going up into space were they fought. People could see bright flashes in the sky from the two connecting blows. The fight dragged on to the face of the moon were they fought for another 29 hours, before god struck Max sending him hurdling like a comet back to earth making a massive explosion in time square. Max was slow to get up, and stagger out of crater he made. God landed next to hole slumped over. They were both exhausted, and wanted the fight to be over with, and they both knew it was going to be done in the next few moves. They knew that one of them was going to make a mistake. So they charged one last time connecting weapons again. They held there for a few seconds before releasing.

God made the first move trying to hit Max with the bottom of his hammer, but Max dodged it. So god lifted his hammer and as he brought his hammer down trying to hit Max on the head Max saw that he left his arm pit open. Max went for it stabbing God, but God, though he was dazed, was still able to bring his hammer down on Max's shoulder braking and crippling Max bringing him to the ground unable to move. God dropped his hammer after the final blow and fell to his knee.

Gods barley able to speak but says "this is impossible??"

Max laying on the ground unable to move complemented, "because you gave me the power dad"

God "you were supposed to help the universe"

Max "I did, look around you. There's peace in the whole of the planet. Yes there was violence, but it was necessary. It had to happen."

God "did you ever attempt to kill one of the demon children in limbo??"

Max "no, I'd never hurt a child of any kind"

God "then that's something Thimblest left out."

Max "no it's not about that. I did what I did because nobody else would do it and I was the one with the ability to do something about it. That's how it's always been. I never like violence, never, but sometimes there's just no way around it, and I'm sorry."

God "no I am sorry, I have failed to see you for who you really are Max."

Max "don't be sorry it was a misunderstanding."

God "no I have to be sorry, I have locked up your wife, started a war with my people who were finally at peace, put you and this planet in an awful position. No I am sorry, and I love you Max"

Max "I love you too dad..." Max watched god collapse to the ground then there was a blinding white light. Max could barely open his eyes, and what Max saw was his arms and half a leg hovering around a blue and black orb the size of a grape fruit. All Max could see beyond the orb was white. Max couldn't tell if there was an end to the whiteness. Max couldn't move at all, and could hardly move his head. He saw that his skin was loose, and his body was that of a boys again floating in the air around the blue orb. Max tried to call out but his voice wouldn't work properly. It was God's voice that responded to him calmly, and greeted Max. Max asked if he could see him. God replied that he could. That Max was in his body. Max asked where he was. God told Max that this is where he was born.

Max asked what the blue orb was. God told Max that it's his creation, where he was born. Max asked how this was possible, and God replied that he sacrificed his a part of his leg to make the orb. Max couldn't believe what he was hearing and through up on himself, and the orb. God told Max to calm down and take a breath. Max started to cry as he realized he could see into the orb. Max told God that he could finally see his family again. God interrupted and told Max to take care of his creation, and then a door opened, and God's voice vanished.

To be cattle

As the door opened Max slowly fell to the ground barley able to move his body. Two elegant blue beings entered the room. They were beautiful in their bodies and in the way they moved. Their hands and feet were missing from evolution, and used backpacks with tubes that ran down their limbs to the missing extremities forming hands and feet out of energy. They were speaking in a language that Max couldn't understand, though their emotions were obvious and suffocated Max's mind, and words didn't need to be said how they felt about him. The vibe they were putting off was that of fresh meat.

They had a hovering flatbed that they loaded Max up on. One of the people grabbed God's orb that was entrusted to Max. Max begged for them to give it back, but all Max could manage was loud whispers. The elegant people didn't seem to care about Max at all, though and continued to bring Max into a different room placing him on a metal table in the middle of what appeared to be an operating room. The one person holding the orb put the orb into a machine then came back to the table to help out the other elegant person. One of them pulled out a knife and started to cut the loose skin away. Max screamed as loud as he could from the pain cracking his voice. The blue person that wasn't cutting yelled at the other cutting, and Max could only get the vibe to be careful with the knife not to falay into the skin.

Once the person was done cutting the loose skin away, and tossing it into a hole in the wall. The other sticks a syringe in Max's arm putting him to sleep. After a few seconds Max falls asleep, and one of the elegant beings walked to the foot of the table and pushes a button making a bar popped out of the bed by Max's feet. The bar had a black bag that it started to cocoon Max in. right as the bar was about to finish another being comes into the room. The first two seemed surprised, and turned to talk to him. But the new being lifted his arm and shot a beam of blue energy from what would be his hand at the two others killing them both. The elegant being quickly grabbed God's orb and placed Max, still in the black bag, onto the hovering flatbed. The being, as fast as he dared without bringing attention to himself, escorted Max to the back of the building where a sky ship was waiting for them. The beings loaded Max, being as gentle as possible, into the ship and took off.

A WHOLE OTHER REALM

Max was slow to wake up, and was still barley able to move. He looked around to see a different elegant being sitting next to him. The man greeted him in Max's language. Max greeted him back politely, and asked where he was. The man told Max that he was in his home village in the sky. Max asked the elegant being who and what he was. The being said that he was a Kelvik, and his name was Sielus. Then Max remember the orb, God's creation, and panicked asking for it. Sielus reached to his left and grabbed the orb gently giving it to Max. Max gently and with great struggle placed the orb on his stomach. Max got a better look at the orb and saw that it was blue with a black mercury type substance swirling in the orb never stopping. Max could feel the orbs inhabitants however he couldn't look inside like he could before, but he could feel the general mood of the whole of the population, and the mood was nervous. Max also sensed the potential for harnessing power from the orb.

Max asks Sielus what all this was about. Sielus told Max that they should talk over a meal. Max agreed that he was pretty hungry, and three Kelviks lifted Max and moved him to a different room with large windows that went directly to the outside showing the sky. The color of the sky reminded Max of gasoline drifting through water. The Kelviks gently set Max onto a cushion with a back, on the ground placing his orb in his lap. Max noticed that his missing leg was back, but he had more important questions he wanted to ask and dismissed it for now. A table barley floating off the ground lay in front of Max with Sielus sitting opposite him.

Strange food was brought out immediately and placed in front of Max. Max reached out with to grab a spoonful of the blue and orange food, but was unable to lift the spoon fully out of the bowl. A Kelvik sat next to Max and started to feed him, which irritated Max. Max asked why he was he was so weak. Sielus told Max that he has never used his body before. That he was bread in that room for a thousand years. Max seemed shocked and had to repeat what Sielus said. Then Max asked why he was in the room in the first place. Sielus looked grim, and confessed that he was part of an ongoing experiment. Max looked at Sielus and asked what kind of experiment. Sielus told Max that he was bread for two reasons. One was for the power of the orb which they used for powering their mighty war machines, and the last was for a food source for royalty.

Max choked a little, and tried to yell out "what did you say?? I was made for meat??" Sielus confirmed Max's outrage. Max's head was a swirl of thoughts and emotions, he put his hand on the table to support his lightheartedness. Sielus asked Max what the orb was and why it had so much important to him. Max still light headed told Sielus that the orb is God's creation placed in his care. Sielus asked who God was. Max told Sielus that God was the previous owner of the body he was in. Which confused Sielus. Sielus asked Max how that's possible.

Max asked if he had time for a story. Sielus nodded, and Max told his story starting from when he first shot himself in his parents' basement. Sielus was captivated by Max story of loss and love. Max could feel Sielus's sadness for him. When Max was done Sielus said that he couldn't fully rap his head around the idea that there were people inside the orb. Max asked unsure if Sielus believed him. Sielus told Max that he used to work for the lab that bread them as a translator, and that he's only talked to one other like him and he said the same thing, then they killed him. Max could feel the Sielus's sadness, as he went on to say how intelligent the other one of his kind were. Perhaps the smartest person he's ever met. Sielus said that he tried to explain his findings to the head of the laboratory, but they wouldn't listen and only fired him for saying what he did. Max asked if there were more of his kind Sielus said that there were 36 more like him at earlier stages of the breeding process.

Max was about to ask a question before a panicked Kelvik came into the room and talked to Sielus. Sielus swore in his language then directed his attention back to Max telling Max that the surface Kelviks were searching the sky villages for him. Max asked how long they had. Sielus told Max a matter of weeks. Max said with confidence that he could learn the power of the orb and save them. Sielus told Max that that was impossible. That the surface Kelviks were ruthless and well-armed. Max said he could do it in exchange for saving him. Sielus again told Max that that was impossible that their flag ship was not to be trifled with, and that their best option was to move Max to a different village. Max said sternly noticing now with more focus on the orb that he could take on their whole fleet. Sielus said more sternly that they were going to move Max.

Max tried making a deal with Sielus that if he gave Max 6 days and he was unable to perform with the orb then they could move him wherever they liked. Sielus thought about it for a few seconds, and Max felt the conflicting emotions in him. Sielus then agreed to the idea. Max could only smile at the craziness in his life how fights always seemed to find him. Sielus asked Max why he was smiling, and Max could only say "it seems no matter where I go. what body I'm in, and no matter how much id like it to be different. I will always be a soldier."

LEARNING TO WALK AGAIN

It took Max three days to learn how to walk again with the help of the Kelviks. Max often got frustrated with himself at how his progress was. He was annoyed at how simple it was, and how hard it was for his body to obey him. the most he could do after six days was an even walk, nothing faster. As for the orb, he unlocked its power after meditating 8 hours a day for five days. The orbs power was limited by its size, and he guessed that the most he could use it before damaging and hurting its inhabitants was about three days of continues use before he had to meditate on it to regain its healthy state.

He also found out he could share a general emotion with the people in the orb in an attempt to sooth, create joy, or In this inevitable case warn them of the upcoming battle. They, in the orb, felt scared by the outside emotion invading their life force. Max did his best to calm down God's creation, however hard it was. He gave them some sort of confidence. Max felt a slight panic that he assumed was the random loss of both God and him. Max focused most of his time with the orb trying to bring peace to it.

The enemy sky fleet showed sooner than the Kelviks thought. With 40 ships ranging from the size of a destroyer, battleship, to even the size of a carrier. They over whelmed the friendly Kelviks with only 12 sky ships the biggest being the size of a small mansion. The real terror was the enemy flagship which was the size of a sky scraper. The Kelviks again told Max that they should run, but Max told them that if he wasn't able to stop them that they could run. There was a small argument between Sielus, Max, and a few other elder Kelviks, but Max won the conversation by telling them to trust him.

The Kelviks were shaking when they lined up their tiny in comparison ships Max being on the biggest ship at the front of the line. As the enemy fleet closed in a smile grew over Max's face as a sinister thought came to him. Max "let the vengeance of my fallen brothers and sisters be my vengeance." Max let go of the orb from his right hand and started to use the power to let it float in front of him. Then used the power of the orb to lift him of the of the sky ship and into the air. Max was held in the air with the orb by outlining himself with a rainbow aura.

Max didn't wait for the ships to get close to the friendly Kelviks, and sped to the fleet. When Max came into range of the ships they opened fire on him. Max, using the orb, deflected every shot and returned his own volley of blue energy at the other ships destroying as many as he could before reaching the flagship. Max landed on the front of the ship using the orb to cut a hole into the ship. Once inside he floated around looking for the orb that powered it. Many Kelviks tried to stop him but Max showed no mercy destroying them.

Max was almost enjoying himself the hate for the people that wanted to eat him and use his home to power weapons tore him from his sanity a little. Max found the orb in a large empty room full of soldiers and in the middle of the room on a pedestal was the orb. The Kelviks emotion was that of terror when Max entered the room, and for good reason. Max erased the Kelviks within a matter of seconds and floated to the orb. Max looked around the red and black swirling orb making sure there were no traps before shrugging and grabbed the orb. Everything on the ship turned off, and the ship started to plummet to the ground. Max made another hole all the way out of the ship, and exited through it.

Once out Max watched as the flagship fell from the sky towards however far the ground was from where he was. The other ships that Max left alone where fighting the Sielus's ships. Max immediately got into the action, taking down one ship after another until they started to retreat. Max wouldn't let them just go and chased after the remaining few destroying the rest. Taking in one last victorious smile Max flew back to the ship that he started on. The Kelviks were in shock at Max's power. Max held out the red and black orb that was a little bigger than his, and told the Kelviks how the surface Kelviks were causing great torment to the orb, and asked Sielus how many other machines they had like that one.

Sielus interrupted Max, and started to yell at him for not letting the enemy retreat. Max grew angry and told Sielus not to yell at him for doing what he thought was justifiably the right course of action considering what he and God's orb was to them. Sielus went quiet for a second then asked if he felt the same about his company. Max shook his head making a face of disgust saying that they saved him. There was no reason for him to hate them. That in fact, he was grateful that they saved him and expressed his humility with a bow placing his fist over his heart. Sielus looked at Max differently and told him to stand. Sielus told Max to try and refrain from killing every last surface Kelvik. Max expressed to Sielus that he would do his best to keep a level head about any situations that arose in the future. Sielus thanked Max.

Max walked closer to Sielus, and asked with a tone of seriousness and confidence that he would like to save the other 36 creators from the lab, and would like it if he could help him. Sielus thought about it for a moment before saying that they could possible get away with it but it would bring war between the sky and the surface which is something that hasn't happened for hundreds of years when they first gained their independence form the surface, though the surface Kelviks still harassed the sky Kelviks by taking money, resources, and even people. Max told Sielus that after today war was already going to happen, and if he had the power to stop that flagship and the other ships, what would the power of another 36 of his kind could do. Sielus looked at the other Kelviks then at the village in the distance then sighed saying "yes, it does not look like I have much of a choice in the matter does it??"

Max smiled and said "I guess not. All I have to say is trust me Sielus. Trust that I'm a good person for the job."

Sielus, "just keep to what we talked about and we will be in agreement." Max held out his hand for Sielus to grab. Sielus took it saying "then an alliance has been formed. Let us bring peace to the land."

Max "one last time."

Going back to the slaughter house

Once back at the village Sielus got a hold of the neighboring villages telling them of Max and what he could do, their plan to get the other children from the lab, and what it could mean for the them the sky villages. A few were eager to get started, but most of them were reluctant and took a lot of persuading. Eventually they got 148 villages to join the cause. Sielus told Max of the opportunity that they had being that they just took out the biggest fleet the surface Kelviks had, and it would be a month before another fleet could make it back from whatever front they were engaged in, and if they left tomorrow they would get to the lab on an off day with few staff members on duty. But it would take 7 days to reach the lab with the fastest ship they had. Max asked how many ships they were taking. Sielus told Max only one and only a few soldiers.

Max seemed surprised and inquired why so few. Sielus reassured Max that there would only be about 16 Kelviks working that day, and none of them are soldiers by any means. Max said excellent and they got the fastest ship they had, ready for the attack. The next day they left early in the morning, if Max had to guess he'd say around 5:30 in the morning. They zoomed as fast as they could, and over the next five days Max meditated to find out if he could find more power in his orb, but to no avail. The power was limited, so Max meditated to find a way of manipulating they orb to do various things which surprised Max at how unlimited a task it could perform. From making water out of air around him, to making a seed that one of the Kelviks gave him grow off of the deck of the ship, and even making a mini sun.

Max tried to learn how to run, but it was still too early in his development accomplish anything more than a faster walk then he could before, which still frustrated him. Max also did his best to warn the inhabitants of the orb about the upcoming fight, but the idea was still nearly impossible to figure out, and left the orb even more distressed then the first time he tried.

When they arrived at the facility at what Max thought was about 10:30 in the morning of the seventh day there was no one in sight. They landed quickly and entered the building just as quick. The soldiers ran up and down the halls subduing or taking out anyone in the building making their way to the breeding rooms. The first room they opened was a blue girl. The girl immediately asked why she couldn't look into her orb and pleaded with the Kelviks to give her orb back. Max walked close to her and told the girl that she and her orb were safe, but she didn't believe Max and continued to plead for the orb. Max knew how she felt and started to tear up telling Sielus that they needed to get the technology to build these rooms and destroy the lab. Sielus told Max that there was only one place in the lab where the information was stored. In the head of staff's office. Max levitated himself and said to lead the way.

Sielus ran towards the direction of the office with Max and four other Kelviks. On the way Max asked how many other labs there were in existence. Sielus told Max that this was the only place that breed them. Max asked why they would only made one, and Sielus told Max that the building was a low key place that only royalty and staff knew about. Their concern was that they didn't want to make it public because then other Kelviks would want a taste of the meat, and the process of breeding takes thousands of years. And to have the enemy know about the orbs would be catastrophic. Max said that that's fine with him, it makes it easier for them to accomplish what they needed to do.

Max asked Sielus why the first girl they saved didn't look like him. Sielus told Max that the only real relation they had together was that they spoke the same language for whatever reason, how they were made, and that most of them created orbs. Otherwise they were made to taste different, and that's where the variety came from. Max grew angry and did his best to control himself for Sielus.

Once at the office Sielus told Max not to take anything the director of the lab says to take to heart. Max asked why, and Sielus tells Max that the head of staff is a cruel man and gains satisfaction from watching his kind cut and taken to the table. Max's face contorted into a snarl. Sielus pleaded with Max not to kill him. Max said he'd try not to. Sielus sighed and opened the door. There standing in front of his desk stood the head of staff. The head of staff greeted Sielus. Sielus greeted him back as Smries. Smries said "so you're the morsel that got away, and what pray tell is your name child??" Max felt Smries smug arrogant confidence, and Max had to hold himself back.

Max "my name is Max"

Smries "it should pain you to know that I already called for help, and they should be here in a matter of moments."

A Kelvik made a move towards Smries, but Max stopped her saying to Smries "why do you eat us, you obviously know we have intelligence."

Smries "when you were created over 700,000 years ago we were impressed by your wisdom, and by the power of your orbs. We offered you a place in our society as soldiers, but many of you declined our ranks, and we didn't mind until you started to claim that there was life in those orbs of yours. HA, impossible. We researched and looked for life and there was nothing, and yet you continued to lie. But in our findings we saw there was potential for power in the orbs, but you wouldn't let us just have your orbs, oh how you cried when we took them away from you. And the power that was wasted on you pathetic pacifists. So we waited for your ancestors to sleep and we slaughtered you in the night, and took the orbs for our own gain."

Max "how are the orbs made??"

Smries "by sacrifice a part of your body of course. The more you sacrifice the bigger the orb. Like the one you took from the Hahst our prized flagship. Oh my, that one was so feisty but you knew that already didn't you Sielus?? That morsel had such a great thing going for you. Learning this barbaric language is not the easiest thing to do in this planet."

Sielus said softly "you're a monster Smries." Smries only laughed smugly.

Max "so when did you start eating us??"

Smries "when we started to breed you for your orbs. It was such a waist to just throw away your carcasses. So we tasted you, and I must say your breed is my favorite, so tell me Max how do you plan to save your people from your continued slavery??"

Max "look for the tech plans for the breeding rooms." Smries lifted his hand to shoot, but Max used the orb to set Smries on fire with blue flames. Smries screamed in agony as he tried to put the flames out with his energy created hands, but to no avail. Sielus let it go for a few seconds more before telling Max to stop. Max obeyed Sielus letting the flames die out. Sielus fell to the ground coughing. Sielus told the others to search for the blueprints.

Smries started to laugh through his coughing saying "you'll never get out of here alive." Max used the orb to mend Smries lips together telling him to shut up. The same Kelvik from earlier said she found the plans. Sielus congratulated her, and said that they needed to get moving. That he was sure they didn't have much time. Sielus asked over his headset if the children were loaded up. The Kelvik on the other end, confirmed that they had the 36 children on the ship. Sielus said excellent and that they were to get the ship started, and that there were reinforcements on the way. The Kelvik was nervous but kept his head saying that they will have the ship ready in a matter of moments.

It took Max's group less than 10 minutes to escape from the building getting aboard the ship, and as quick as they could took off. Just as they cleared some distance from the facility several vehicles drove around the building shooting at the ship, but the ship was out of range. Max looked over the edge of the ship and shot a massive beam of blue energy from the orb destroying the lab with one shot. An hour after they cleared some distance from the lab a fleet of ships came into view. Sielus swore in his language and told Max that that was the 5th fleet. Max asked, bewildered by the size of the fleet, how they got to them so quickly. Sielus told Max that they must have been refueling from the battle front just north of the compound. The ships were a lot smaller than the fleet Max fought a few days ago, but they numbered almost 180. Max grew serious and told Sielus that he'll take care of them when they get closer, and that there's nothing to worry about.

It was about 2:00 pm when the fleet came into range, and started shooting. Max held a blue transparent bubble around the ship before flying towards the ship and shooting them down. Max constantly had to stay close to the ship to protect it from fire, engaging which ever ship came close enough that Max could shoot accurately. Three hours into the fight the enemy ships started to back off giving Max's ship some room. Max stayed close to the ship after that keeping in communication with Sielus with a headset. The two agreed that the fleet was waiting for night to attack again. so Max came back to the ship and asked how his brothers and sisters were doing. Sielus told him that many were confused, and the rest were irritated that they were unable to see into their orbs.

Max asked if they all had their own orbs. Sielus said that they do, and many of the creators were being rude demanding things from Sielus constantly with no respect for the sacrifices they made to save them. Max apologized for them being so rude. Sielus said that it was ok, and that he had a gift for Max. Max got excited and asked what it was. Sielus told him that while they were storming the lab they were able to take a few lab workers prisoner, and they agree to help build the rooms for them simply to keep working at the job. Max said excellent, and that he couldn't wait to create and army to help the sky villages. Sielus reminded Max of how long it took to breed just one creator. Max sighed and looked into the distance and said that then all the sky Kelviks have are just the 36 of them. Sielus cringed a little stating that he doesn't even think that many of them will fight. Max sighed right after him apologizing once again for what he got Sielus and his people into, and how he hopes some of the creators will make it worth their time.

Sielus turned the conversation to Max's orb asking how much power it had left. Max told Sielus that it could last until tomorrow and towards the beginning of the of the day after tomorrow, but there would still be more than enough ships he figured by that time especially because he couldn't take the time to focus on meditating with the orb while the ships could still sneak up on them during the day. Sielus agreed that he had to be vigilant. Then one of the Kelviks stormed up to Sielus and started to rage in his own language at Sielus. Max and Sielus patiently waited for the Kelvik to finish before telling Max that one of his brothers is demanding to know where they were going, and asked for Sielus personally. Max just sighed and shook his head asking if he should go with him. Sielus told Max that he need to stand guard on the deck. Max agreed and told Sielus good luck. Sielus made a face of indifference and sighed turning in the direction of the stairs leading below deck. Max turned and notice a ship creeping up below their ship and Max went to work.

It was around 10 when the action happened. It was more intense fighting then the day time and it was a lot harder to find the ships in the darkness. So after a while Max came back to the ship and focus on protecting the ship with the blue bubble he made around the it. Max stayed up all night holding the bubble. At the first sign of light Max started his attack tired as he was, he fought the enemy ships until they retreated back to the distance they held the day before. Max flew back to the ship and landed with a hard thump. Sielus asked if he was going to be ok for the next two or more days, or however long this took. Max could barely stay awake from the exhaustion. Max smiled and told Sielus about how he once stayed up for two months just for the heck of it now he could barely do two days, and ended his reply with a no he wouldn't be able to last for much longer.

Sielus grew very worried. Max asked if the ship could go any faster. Sielus said that it has been pushed to the limits and he was surprised that the ship hasn't broken down yet leaving them stranded in the air. Max remembered the creators and asked Sielus if one of the creators had found their orbs power yet. Sielus remembered too and said that he would be right back. Max fell to both knees leaning back onto his heels, and waited for Sielus to get back. His eyes grew cobwebs and he started to drift into a slumber for a little bit before Sielus returned with one Kelviks carrying one of the creators. The Kelviks gently set the creator next to Max who quickly snapped out of it. Sielus told Max who was slowly getting to his feet that the creator he brought was the only one that could use there orbs in a somewhat of an efficient way.

The creator was blue with pointed ears and black eyes, her orb was a little smaller then Max's with orange swirls and tiny purple squares floating randomly in it. she was missing her right four arm, and Max knew what that meant. Max greeted the girl and the girl greeted him back. Max asked for her name and she replied that it was Flay. Flay smiled and asked if he was the one that saved them with the help of the Kelviks. Max blushed and said that it was no big deal. Flay got serious and look past through the railing at the still many ships that were chasing them, and said "so that is what's chasing us. Curious as we were about the mysterious lights and loud cracks of sound that followed. So how can I help you??" Max asked how well she could use her orb like if she could fly and shoot down the other ships. Flay told Max that if she could do all of that she still wouldn't, and that she was a pacifist.

Max laughed a little not knowing how to react to what was just said and replied "what??" Flay smiled back at Max and asked if he knew what pacifist was. Max's face dropped and wiped his hands across his face looking up to the sky saying "you have to be kidding me" looking back at Flay. Flay was I little displeased and told Max that he didn't need to be rude. Max apologized saying that they were going to be killed or captured, and then maybe after that then they'd be killed. Flay excepted the apology and stated that she could simply make the ship move faster than the other ships if that help. Max felt really stupid saying how perfect that was. Flay smiled saying how different he was form the other creators. Max told her that he wasn't a creator, and that he just took his creators place over strange happenings.

Flay raised an eyebrow that was covered by the extra coat of flesh that covered all the creators, and asked how that was possible. Sielus interrupted and told them that they needed to focus on the task at hand. They both agreed with Sielus and they came up with a game plan. Max was going to sleep for as many hours as Flay would let him. Then Max would come out and fly after the ships taking as many down as possible before night. Then when night hit Flay and Max would switch from protecting the ship and speeding the ship up to get the distance going. But that was it, they only had the one plan for that day until morning. They didn't know if they could last the next day, but they decided to figure that out tomorrow. And so for the next four hours while Max slept Flay would boost the ship if any of the enemy got close to them. when Flays orb was getting tired she had Sielus go wake Max.

Max grudgingly got out of the bed they made for him with the mindset that he didn't want to do anything. So when he got to the back of the ship he greeted Flay but didn't wait for her to say anything back before flying out and taking care of the enemy. Flay mentioned how rude that was to Sielus, and Sielus told her that that's how he was every time they woke him up, and that he would sleep for nearly 9 or 10 hours if they didn't wake him. Flay smiled and said that he really wasn't a creator. Sielus asked how it was possible to have created life in such a small ball that looked like it only held liquid. Flay told Sielus the whole orb was organic and living. the shell was the outer most part of the orb, the part that he can touch. And beyond the shell if he could look past the swirling life energy that she and what she assumes every creator uses to make life from, their sacrificed limb, was a whole universe that existed in the center of it.

Sielus couldn't believe what he just heard, and asked if that's what happens when she sacrificed that part of her arm that she was missing. Flay nodded saying that it took most of her life to make the orb from the small portion that she used and how painful it was to give birth to life, and that's why she cares about the orb so much. Sielus said "strange then that Max has such a passion for his orb. From what he told me he hated his creator before he slayed him." Flay shook her head as fast as she could bewildered asking if he was telling the truth. Sielus told her that that's what Max told him, but quickly said that his creator and him made up before they were separated. Flay got serious and asked Sielus what else Max told him. Sielus told Flay that he already said to much, and it wasn't his place to be telling someones personal story.

Flay crossed her arm with her stump, and said "he has a lot of explaining to do."

Sielus smiled and replied "I think you will be impressed by him Flay. He has been through a lot for what seems like forever for him, and he has had nothing but time to call his teacher."

Flay smiled slightly saying "then I am interested to hear what he has to say" the both watched as in the distance all they could see was small dots shooting blue and red lines at each other.

It was the dying rays of light that finally brought Max back. landing on the ship feeling pleased with the progress he made. He sat leaning back on both hands putting one knee up and resting the other flat on the ground, asking how she was doing. Flay said she was doing well enough and asked how he was doing. Max replied that he was tired, but he was still ready for the night. Flay asked Max if he did a lot of fighting as the created. Max replied that he did what no one else was willing to do and that it always led to more violence, and how people on his home planet were never satisfied with what they had always taking more then they needed. Max went on to say how frustrated it made him that it took him to the point of changing into something even more violent and powerful then the rest of the people on his plant to scare them into making peace.

Flay told Max that Sielus told her that he killed his creator and asked why. Max told her that it was a very long story, and if they made it to the sky village he would tell all the his brothers and sisters, and that they had to pay attention to the task at hand. Flay agreed that it could wait. Max asked Flay if she could go first and speed the ship up that his orb was getting warn out. Flay smiled and said it would be her pleasure. For the rest of the night Flay would keep the ship at a distance only stopping to keep her orb with sufficient power to perform for the rest of the night. while the other part of then night when the ships came close Max would shield the ship from the enemies blasts. They had brakes in between the time when Flay stopped speeding the ship and the enemy catching up to them. That time was filled with small talk getting to know one another and meditating on their orbs.

Flay mostly asked what God was like. Max would tell her that he was stern, focused, kind, wise, strong, and many other things before he decided to dumb it down by calling him a dad for many parts. Flay asked if what he looked like and Max asked if she meant outside of the orb or in this universe. Flay asked both. Max told her that he had his body in this universe so that's what he would look like, but in the other world his looks were that of a broad tall stance back straight, a white beard mid length perfectly trimmed, and the first time he saw him he was wearing blue robes with white and gold trim, and the second time at the fight he ware only a few gold plates of armor and a solid white robe underneath the armor. Flay would say how dreamy he must have been. Max would smirk saying how wired it was to hear a creator being infatuated with God, and Max guessed that Flay was blushing, though, he couldn't tell do to the loos skin covering her body.

The other part of the night was filled with techniques for Flay on how to use her orb more efficiently. By the end of the night they were both exhausted and needed sleep. But Max flew out anyways and got the ships off their back for the day only taking a few of them out and scaring the rest to safe distance. When he landed back on the deck Sielus greeted Flay and him bringing them the equivalent of coffee and asked how the night went. They both told him that it went well for the most part but now they both needed sleep and had to meditate on their orbs to bring its power back. Sielus suggested that they ask for another creator to help though he didn't know if any of them were ready. Flay and Max both agreed that there was no other option. Sielus started to walk in the direction of the stairs but Max asked Flay if she could hold down the ship while he went with Sielus. Flay nodded and Max thanked her saying he won't be long. Flay joked and said "you better not be" Max smiled and went with Sielus below deck.

Sielus led Max to the room where the creators were staying. Sielus opened the door and instantly there were loud whisper of hatred, regret, and nothing else that was kind directed at Sielus. Sielus sighed and dragged his hand of energy across his body for Max to see what he saved. Max walked into the room to see many different types of beings all with anger on their face save for 6 of them. They grew very quiet when Max entered the room. Max greeted them with genuine respect, but only the 6 not with hate on their face greeted him back. one of the creators green with scales on his body asked as rude as he could what he wanted. Max held both hands up as if to ease them, and told them the situation they were having above deck and if any of them would help with their orb. Immediately they started yelling in whispers telling him to go away that they didn't have anyone else.

Max held his hands up again and said that if they don't escape the ships that were chasing them they would all be killed, eaten, and their orbs be used for horrible uses until it eventually died from exhaustion. They all quieted, and the green scaly creator from before asked if it was true. Max told them that the lab they just came from breeds them for their orb and uses their bodies as food, and those are the people chasing them. They all grumbled and said fine. The green creator said that he was able to use his orb for what it's worth, and asked how long he'd have to use it. Max said he would have to talk to both Flay and him to come up with a plan. The green creator grumbled and said with no patience that he needed someone to carry him up.

Sielus sighed again picking up the green scaled child. Max thanked him but the creator only waved his hand and huffed. Once up top Sielus set the green creator down next to Flay. Flay didn't even greet the green boy knowing how rude he was to her earlier. Max asked what his name was. The creator replied that his name was Rubex. Max commented on how he like Rubex's name trying to lighten the mood, but Rubex again waved his hand and said to get on with what he must do. Flay had been thinking about it while Max was away and asked Rubex if he could speed the ship up for at least two ours. Rubex grunted and said smugly "is that all you want??"

Flay got irritated and asked "well then how about four hours??" Rubex sniffed and said fine that he could do it. Flay said great sarcastically and asked Max if he could charge his orb after he slept for the four hours given. Max said that he would have to meditate for at least an hour before he could take down the last few ships. Flay said excellent and that she would sleep for two hours and meditate for the last two hours and use her orb to speed the ship up until Max had his orb ready to go. They all agreed on the plan, and Sielus helped Flay to a room while Max went to that same room from before. Rubex sat alone for the next two hours keeping the ship away from the other enemy ships.

Sielus woke Flay up around 8 in the morning, and carried her to where she sat last time. Rubex didn't even greet her. Flay just ignored him and went right to meditating for the next two hours until Max was woken up, and in the same mood as the day before and in the exact same way greeted the two of the sat down and meditated. Rubex asked why he was being so rude. Flay just shook her head as she took over for Rubex. Rubex sat there and watched the two work. Rubex asked Flay how she was able to use her orb so well after the few days she had been out of their room. Flay said that she was concentrating. Rubex huffed and crossed his arms.

About an hour and 15 minutes later Max stood up and without saying anything flew towards the enemy and started to do work on them. Flay relaxed and started to drift in and out of sleep. Rubex demanded to know who Max was and how he could use his orb so well. Flay said that it was none of his business and he should be grateful that he saved his life. Rubex asked why she would deafened him and asked what they talked about over the night. Flay told Rubex that it wasn't her place to tell anything about Max and that he didn't even tell her his whole story. Rubex asked why she was so incompetent, and told her that she was going to be excluded with the other six that refuse to co-operate with the rest of the creators.

Flay simply told Rubex quoting Max, "its whatever" Rubex was taken back but shut up. Sielus joined Flay and Rubex and together, they watched Max make short work of the rest of the ships and three hours later Max returned to the ship and landed in front of the three sitting down cross legged immediately. Sielus complemented the three for the good work and how they all would have been put on the chopping block had it not been for them. Max thanked Flay and Rubex for their help. Flay thanked Max back. Rubex grunted and asked how he was able to do so much with his orb. Max smiled and told Rubex that if he's nice he'll show him. Flay laughed knowing Max's secret that he was a simple life form. Rubex demanded that Max tell them what he knows. Max told Rubex to chill out. Rubex couldn't believe what he heard.

This went on for several minutes before Flay worked through her laughter and asked Max what his story was now that they had the time. Max said fine, and started telling his story starting from the time he shot himself in his parents' basement for the hundredth time. At the end of it both creators were speechless. Flay was the first to speak saying how impressed she was that he accomplished so much in the little bit of time that he was alive. How he was able to come to terms with God and both realizing the love they had and the mistakes they made and just what his home was and what he turned it into before destroying everything looking for a way to see his loved ones.

Rubex however was appalled at Max for killing his creator saying that he should have just let God kill Max. Rubex demanded that Sielus take him back to the other creators and determine how they felt about Max. Sielus gave Max a look of despair knowing over the last three days what the creators were all about. As Sielus carried Rubex away Flay put a hand on Max's arm saying that she'll protect him from the other creators. Max thanked her and said he'd do anything for his brothers and sisters. Flay smiled awkwardly and asked again what he called the creators. Max repeated himself feeling now foolish about it. Flay asked why he called them that. Max told her that they were all born the same way speak the same language why wouldn't they be related??

Flay giggled and said "I guess so. I just wish I had my normal body again the body I created in my universe. It was so beautiful. Now I'm just a flimsy skinned child."

Max told her "don't worry about the skin it comes off, but I hope there's an easier way to get it off. The Kelviks in the lab just cut it all off. It was so painful I could barely stand it, and the worst part is I hurt my voice trying to yell." Flay looked distressed asking if that was going to be her fate?? Max nodded and told her about how they were going to be used as food for royalty and the orbs for powering war machines. Flay got a little light headed and asked who would do such a thing to a living creature. Max felt weird saying that he eats livestock but he feels that some animals are there for eating why else would they give so much nutrition?? Flay commented that in her universe she made vegetation produce have an abundance of nutrition and every creature ate from the plants as did she. Flay asked if it was the same for his home. Max replied that he never made it off his planet so the vegetation gave only a little benefits in some places and a lot in others so as far as protein goes meat was the best option.

Though there were people that devoted their lives to only eating vegetables and fruit and that he thought that was admirable. Flay laughed saying how odd he was for wanting to live one way and saying that another life style was just as good. Max looked at her with a smile and thanked her awkwardly not sure how to take that. Flay looked at Max and thanked him for being what he was for the state in which he was raised. Flay looked at the sky and asked if there was really that much violence and hate where he came from. Max sighed and said that people were so caught up in themselves that the few people that wanted freedom from the hate had nowhere to go. Some protested but got nowhere, others fought but were often defeated by the person with the bigger stick.

Max "many people lost hope, others accepted it, and the ones fighting gained no ground. Everything seemed hopeless. Then God and Lucifer gave me the seeds and I was back on earth with no purpose until I met Zoey. And the first time she got shot I didn't want to see the violence anymore, but it was her plan to save the world. I agreed and followed her lead. It was terrible how people got so greedy that they kept taking and leaving nothing for the common person. The worst part was there were so few people that wanted to make a difference that nothing would ever get done. So I'm happy I got involved because I was the only one with the power to change the world." Sielus came and sat next to them.

Flay commented to Max "and the worst part about all of it is that even when you tried to help one person another got jealous and wanted you to help them. Your home must have been a mess. Why didn't God step in??"

Just then a beautiful cat with wings of swirling energy landed on the railing of the ship in front of them saying "that's what Max was for. He was supposed to change his planet and give them hope, and when he did all I saw was and an unfocused monster. For that I'm sorry Max."

Max stood up as quick as he could saying excitedly "God??"

The cat looked at Max unblinking and started grooming his head with his paw saying "yes Max it is me and I am happy for what you did for my kind. However I am still displeased with how violent and vengeful you were. You are lucky to have Sielus as a friend to level your head out."

Flay and Sielus looked astonished Flay saying "so you're the rumored creator I have been hearing so much about. Well I can say that you are not as handsome as I thought." Flay laughed jokingly.

God said jokingly though you couldn't tell by his cat face and the tone in his voice "well now I can say from what Hyperion showed me of you, you were indeed as beautiful as you mentioned to Max." Sielus stood up immediately asking God if he really met Hyperion. Flay asked who Hyperion was. Sielus told her that Hyperion was the deity that created the planet they live in.

Flay and Max said together "live in??"

Sielus staggered on his sentence saying "yea he lives on the outside of the planet." Max commented that the planet was outside in. Sielus replied saying "is not the same for your homes??" Flay and Max looked at each other and back at Sielus saying no.

Flay asked "well then how does your sun turn dark during the night??" Sielus told her that the sun only glowed that brightly during the day and at night the dim side of the sun faced them. Max said how strange that was not to be rude just out of curiosity, and that Heaven and Hell was set up that way but he thought that was still weird. Flay asked just how far away the sun was from them.

Sielus told them "well it is not in the exact middle of the planet. About 94 trillion kilometers when its further from us." Flay and Max's faces looked surprised. Max asked how big the planet really was. Sielus told them that the planet was 196 trillion kilometers exactly at any point of the plant from the other.

Max shook his head not believing what he heard saying "ok how did you know it was that exact number??" Sielus smiled saying that they measured it many times over the recorded septillion years they have existed. Flay commented on how old their civilization is saying that very few species could survive on a planet outside of a solar system.

God commented saying "that's why Hyperion made it this way. The planet is completely self-reliant until the resources are depleted then he starts over. That's why it's so big and has lasted so long. It was made for this." Max asked Sielus if they have ever dug to the other side before.

Sielus told Max "we started to dig 500,000 years before we started to breed you. Then after your attempt to rise against the land kelviks they started using your orbs for a drill. We have been drilling ever sense." Flay asked how deep the hole was. Sielus told her that they stopped counting but it takes several months to get out from the bottom, and protective gear is needed to take the plunge.

God interrupted saying "that's where you and the other 6 creators have to go. The realm of gods is on the other side of the planets crust. Hyperion waits for you there." Flay and Max asked God what he meant by the other 6. God told them that the other creators have decided that Max is a useless life form whose only purpose now is to teach them how to use their orbs. Max clenched his fist, but God calmed him down with soothing words of comfort in manner of hope telling him that Hyperion has a gift for him and the other 7. Flay asked God what he meant by the other creators. God told them that there were a few creators that opposed the majority and have been exiled from the group. Sielus took over confirming what God said that that's why he came up was to tell them what God just finished telling them.

Max leaned against the railing of the ship and said "well shit don't they even care what I did for them??" Flay said that she wouldn't expect anything less from the other creators. Max looked at God asking what they should do.

God told Max "I am sorry to leave you like this Max but my task is over. I take my leave knowing that I can live without responsibility until the time Hyperion aloud me runs out. Then I will fade like the rest of my children in the whispers of time taking the final rest." Flay commented on how envious she was of him. God continued to say "I am sorry Max that I would ever let Lucifer build such a horrible place for my damned children to spend the rest of eternity. I love you Max. you are my greatest mistake." Max blushed not knowing how to take that, and thanked God. God finished saying to Max "just promise me that you will bring back Jesus, the angels you killed, and Lucifer back from oblivion."

Max nodded promising but then said to God "I can't even look into your orb"

God replied "it is your orb now take care of it as if it were an extension of your own body Max. Love it as I did."

God turned to leave but Flay stopped god and asked "what is your mortal name creator??"

God looked back at Flay and said "my mortal name is of no importance given this stage of my life as I drift through this world as an alien creature native only in the world that I created. I take my leave from everything I was and held dear to me, and now begins my life anew with true freedom." And with that God took flight and was gone. Max watched God fly away until he was nothing but sky.

Max turned to Sielus and asked if he knew where the hole was that the land Kelviks were digging. Sielus said that he did that it would only take a month and a few weeks to get there. Max looked at both Flay and Sielus saying "take me to the exiled creators." Flay and Sielus both smiled with Max's air of confidence. Max looked back at where God was before the distance took him and said "thanks dad I will not fail you a second time, and I love you too."

THE PLAN

Sielus picked up Flay preparing for what comes next. The three made their way down below through the halls of the ship and into the room that held the creators to see for their self what God was talking about. Max opened the door to glares from all the brothers and sisters sitting in their designated spots they gave themselves. Sielus helped Flay into her spot and walked over to the door where Max was leaning against the door frame. Rubex spoke on behalf of the children creators. Rubex started by saying that Max will not nor will ever be their equals. Rubex "that being said, you are to help us figure out how to use our orbs power in a more efficient way. Do you understand??"

Max "well that being said what if I don't want to help you ungrateful pricks??" The entire room turned into loud whispers and soft voices cursing Max and demeaning him. Max smiled which made it worse. Flay held her hand up trying to calm them down asking them to hear her out. When the room was quiet Flay opened by saying how Max helped them escape from a terrible fate, and saved them from that continued fate, and for that they should be thanking him. Another sister told her that she has been twisted by Max's words and would only help Max bring a down the fall to their race, that Rubex told them how she defended him against Rubex. A few other creators agreed with the sister.

A brother suggested that she go to the other room with the other exiled creators. The other creators all agreed with the brother that Flay was of no use to them. Flay was baffled by their quick to judge attitude, and how incredibly childish they were being. Flay flagged down Sielus to move here to the room with the other creators that were also banished from the brothers and sisters. Sielus picked up Flay and carried her out of the room down the hall leaving Max to the mercy of the other creators.

Rubex was the first to say something demanding again to Max that he show them how to use their orbs better. Max again asked why he should help them when they were being rude about it. whispers of insults flew at Max again. Max explained to them that that wasn't going to help change his mind. Rubex called him incompetent and said if he didn't help them they would forever make him an outcast in their society. Max smiled and said saying that he would help them if they would treat him with respect. A sister told Max that he was nothing to them. Max asked them why they were being so mean without a real reason. Just as he asked that Sielus entered the room. Rubex spoke for all of them telling him that if he was willing to kill his creator then what was stopping him from destroying them. Max started to say that he spoke to God, but Sielus quickly stopped him telling him that the exiled children need to speak with him.

Rubex said that that'd be a good idea that maybe seeing how weak the other creators were that maybe Max would agree to help them instead. Max sniffed and said that it would be a good idea and that they had better calm down and speak to him with some manners when he gets back. The creators said something to the effect of not really. Max just shook his head and left the creators to their bull shit. Sielus lead the way to a room at the end of the hall.

When Sielus opened the door for Max he saw 7 child creators including Flay. The creators all greeted Max, Max greeted them back thanking them for their kindness after the bombardment of insults he just received. Flay began to introduce the creators starting with Agront (Agront was the color black with white hair, and solid white eyes. His orb was blue with purple circles, and inside the circles were orange squares. His orb was a little bigger then Max's), Suist (she looked like a human but her hair was a dark shade of green, and her eyes were orange and green with no pupils. Her teeth were razor sharp. Her orb was smaller than Max's was, a light shade of purple with dark purple swirls), Barnet (he had a gray skin tone, though you couldn't see it under the lose skin but he had glowing aqua tribal lines. His hair was aqua, with aqua glowing eyes. His orb was roughly the same size as Max's, it was green with a black shifting tree in the middle.), Zleist (also black as Agront, like the shade black, with purple hair and an orange streak going down her left side. Her eyes were white with green irises and blue pupils, and long slim ears. Her orb about the same size as Flays, red with black and yellow triangles floating around inside.), Marex (her skin tone was solid white, with again you couldn't see it with the lose skin covering her body, but a red stripe going down the middle of her body. Her hair was white with white glowing eyes and glowing red pupils. Her orb was pink with black swirls.), Ehwest (her skin tone was white the shade white like Marex. Blue hair and once more do to the lose skin covering her she had blue upside down triangles under her eyes, and blue lips. Her ears were longer and pointer then Zleist. her sclera was glowing blue no irises and black pupils. Her orb was the smallest of the 8 (including Max's). Her orb was white with black "o's" in the middle.).

Max greeted them again, and asked if Flay told them about what God said. Flay said that she informed them and they were in the midst of talking about the other council. Barnet started saying that the other creators were not to be trusted. He had an obvious distaste for them. Suist also agreed with Barnet though not as much hate in her voice. Ehwest asked Max if he said anything about God or what God asked for them to do, to the other creators. Sielus interrupted saying that he stopped Max before he could divulge anything to them. There was a sigh of relief in the room. Agront commented that about what Sielus said once about Max talking too much, and laughed a little. Marex giggled a little saying that she liked the way Max spoke, and that he reminds her of one of her favorite creations.

Ehwset told Marex that that wasn't important. Marex said that she needs to, trying to speak like Max, lighten up. Ehwest just shook her head saying how ridiculous she is. Barnet told them to stay focused to the task at hand. Marex and Ehwest agreed, and the conversation continued to where the dig site was and how they were going to keep this information away from the untrustworthy creators in the other room. They talked for several minutes, but came up short.

Then Max said finally "we could fake like we took a life boat back to the surface, so the other brothers and sisters think we left the ship. Then when we get to the village they will unload the other brothers and sisters while loading supplies to make a camp and the building supplies to make the white rooms for more siblings. Once we get loaded up we can make our way down to the surface making camp a few miles from the dig site. We can tell the other brothers and sisters that you Sielus and a group of other Kelviks are going to take this ship out to look for us. But one thing Sielus do you have life boats on this ship right??"

Sielus said that they do have what he thinks he would call a life boat. Flay asked Sielus if the land Kelviks they captured would help them build the white rooms. Sielus told the group that they would being that they were so dedicated to the job and they were colleges of his before he left the job. Max asked if it sounded like a plan to them. they discussed a few more cogs in the plan before they all agreed with Max's plan. Sielus said that he would tell the other creators what happened and how one of the life boats were missing but in actuality a few Kelviks took it to the village.

As Sielus was leaving Marex asked Max why he called the creators brothers and sisters, and that they had no real relationship with each other. Max told them that it's because they were all made the same way and he was their big brother, because he was born first. The group chuckled a little, making Max blush and smile a little feeling silly. Marex said that she liked the idea. Flay and Suist agreed with her. Agront agreed because it made a little sense. The others just simply agreed. Max was enlightened by how weird that now sounded. Marex said "ok then we will now be called the council of the first family. Agreed??" Agront grunted that he agreed. Barnet crossed his arms saying that it was different but he agreed. Suist and Flay agreed with it almost instantly. Zleist made no real emotion and instead agreed not to conform but because it was something they could call themselves to separate them from the other creators. Max said that it sounded pretty cool, and Ehwest told Marex that that was the first thing she said that made some sense.

Barnet said with some importance in his voice "then let it be known that we are now the first family. May our fortune be nothing but perfect, our lives last long enough for the mission to be carried out, and our enemies know that we are to be feared."

ATTACK ON THE DIG SITE

Sielus came back to the room after several hours. The first family had been asking Max about his adventures from his former life. They were rather impressed with what his story was. when Sielus entered the room he seemed to have a chip on his shoulder as big as his smile. The group looked at him awkwardly smiling now at his demeanor and asking Sielus why he was so happy thinking that the talk with the other creators would have sent him back angry and frustrated. Sielus told them that they took the information with grate hatred for their small group, and how if they ever found the First Family they would kill them all in different but equally painful ways. Agront asked Sielus why that was so funny. Sielus told them that they should have seen their faces when he told them the news. Sielus told the group that they started to blame everyone including themselves, and insulting the first person that said anything about the first family. The group laughed at the thought of the whispering creators.

Barnet stopped the humor by asking Sielus if they let one of the safety boats go. Sielus told them that they had a crew leave about 15 minutes after he left the room. He also told the group that he warned the village of what was about to come to their home, and to get preparations to for the trip to the surface. the group thanked Sielus for the work and taking the insults from the other creators. Sielus said he was happy to help. For the remainder of the trip Max tout the group how to use their orbs effectively. When they arrived at the village they stayed in the room, and waited for the Kelviks to finish what they were doing. Max looked out the window of the of the room and saw that there were hundreds of different villages surrounding the original sky village which excited him knowing that there were so many that wanted to stand up to the surface. About an hour later the ship took off towards the surface of the planet.

Sielus came back into the room and had Max helped move the creators into a room with two metal beds with an arm at the foot of the bed. Sielus had Max put two the children on either bed and he started to push buttons on a control panel in between the beds. When Sielus push the last button the arms at the end of the beds started to move up the their bodies and began to mend the missing appendages and removing the lose skin. The creators felt no discomfort. Max said that he wish his skin was removed that way and explained how terrible it felt when the Kelviks at the lab removed his skin from his body. A few of the creators cringed at the idea and were thankful to Max for saving them from the fate.

One by one the creators were turned into their real state. Thankful to Sielus they moved their bodies checking themselves out in a mirror at the back of the room. Once finished they started to train more on their orbs and learning to walk. Max laughed at Zliets because in her orb she never walked, and learning to was very difficult to her, trying to understand how it worked took several days. By the time they arrived at what they dubbed a strategic place for camp (at a place where there shouldn't be any traffic to/from the dig site and no homes, villages, or any life other than wild animals for thousands of miles other than the dig site which was roughly 100 miles away), the group could walk and use their orb just as well as Max. once they landed they immediately started unloading the ship and setting up camp making domes instead of tents.

With the help of the first family the camp was built in no time. After the camp was set up and the crew ate supper, the 8, Sielus, and a Kelvik that had worked at the dig sight for a few years as a slave before escaping, started making plans for the attack on the dig site. The man that had worked there informed the group how many people should be working there if it was still the same, and where the orb that powered the massive drill was located. The man told them that it was the beginning of the month and that they just started a new shift so there shouldn't be anyone coming to the dig site unexpectedly. They planned for hours making sure everything would go smoothly. When they were satisfied with what they had planned they retired to their domes and prepared for the next day.

When the 8 woke up the Kelviks had already started building the white room to make more creators. The Kelviks had supplies for the 8 already to go in backpacks. Sielus and a few other Kelviks not working said their good byes and wished the 8 the best of luck, and they were of into the unknown. They flew for several hours before stopping just out of the dig site. They stopped to meditate on their orbs to recharge them and eat something. It was about noon when they took up positions just high in the sky that they wouldn't be noticed making a perfect circle around the site. When they were ready they signaled each other, and then it started.

Flay took out all the communication towers as told by the man that worked there. And the rest started taking out the people on the ground, though Flay didn't like the idea of killing them. the process took only an hour to accomplish. Once they were finished they looked for the orb powering the drill which was right were the worker told them it would be. They put out the fires so as to not bring any unwanted attention. Then they made their way down the massive hole. Astonished by how fare down the hole was they dropped for miles and miles needing to stop numerous times. Total they traveled for three weeks trying to get to the bottom stopping to rest only when they had to. Once they reached the bottom they started to use their orbs to dig. They dug for months. They would dig for days on end trying reach the outside of the planet, resting and sleeping for only a few hours save when they had to meditate on their orbs. it had been three months and one week before they blasted their way out of the crust and into blackness.

THE REALM OF GODS

They had done it, they finally made their way out of the hole and looked around into the darkness the that enveloped them with only the light of their orbs to guide them. The air was hot and stuffy. There was a loud but still distant melody being hummed. Zliest asked confused where Hyperion was. Marex asked next if they would even be able to find him.

Agront told them they wouldn't find him by floating around, and they agreed to start looking but together as to not get lost from each other given the dark emptiness of the area. They started to fly in one direction when a yellow light showed and a massive hand the size of the Atlantic Ocean lifted from under them carrying them up with such force they even with the orb couldn't stay standing, and remained pressed against the palm.

It took 20 minutes before the hand stop in front of a man the size of a planet. He was sitting with his legs crossed floating in the black ibis with a yellow aura surrounding him. His skin tone was brown with black hair and beard that reached over his massive belly and onto his feet. His eyes glowed white. He ware white robes with gold and blue trim and a gold circlet around his head. None of the 8 could believe what they were seeing.

Hyperion spoke to Max first saying a booming voice "Max you have come a long way to be in the position you are in, and I am very impressed by your deeds. I have asked you to come to me for a reason you see. I thank the rest of you my children for helping Max reach the realm of gods to talk to me. I know it took a lot of courage for you to turn your backs on your equals." No one knew what to say or if they should say anything at all. Hyperion let out an earth shattering laugh with such force the 8 had to use their orbs to keep themselves in one spot. Hyperion spoke again "go on children don't be intimidated, go on speak" he said with a smile.

Flay spoke first saying "thank you Hyperion for giving us such an honorable and unbelievable opportunity to speak with you."

Hyperion "in the entire time I have spent creating worlds, which this is the sixth one, you 8 are the first of my children I have let speak or even see me. I love all my children but you eight, especially you Max, have gone through so much that I see your importance to me. I love you and I can say that the comical relationship between you Ehwest and Marex is only rivaled by the romantic love Max has for Zoey and the father son relationship with Jacob. And for your stories I have more love for you 8 then I do for any of my other children now and in the past. Your stories are the best I have ever had the joy of watching."

Max said bluntly "so why are we here dad??"

Hyperion let out another bellowing laugh with the same effect and said "that's why I love you most Max you have no sense of a higher being and so you speak what is on your mind only acknowledging your situation and nothing else, and you fear nothing not even the power in front of you. I asked for you all to be here because knowledge is infinite just like the gods who created it, and I am going to teach you that knowledge Max. all I ask is that you stay with me until my time has come, and that you give me the same love that you give my children around me."

Barnet asked "you will die great creator??"

Hyperion "no, there is no end and always a beginning. My body will soon disappear from the realm of gods, and my life force be given back to the empty space around you until our mother gives birth to me again like all her children. When that time comes I will have taught you everything I know Max. Then you Max will take up my mantel and look after my creation. Would you like this title my child??"

Max thought about it for a second then asked "will the first family be able to stay??"

Hyperion "no, but they may visit as much as they would like. No, they are going to be busy for the remainder their time spent in my creation, if they choose to help my Kelviks."

Agront "are they in danger Hyperion??"

Hyperion got solemn "your suspicions of your equals is true Barnet. They plan to conquer all the of my creation."

Barnet crossed his arms with a grim face said "I knew they were no good."

Ehwest "but we lack the strength to fight them great Hyperion. How could we make a difference??"

Hyperion smiled and put a finger to the side of his nose and said "I know this to be true Ehwest. This is why I am giving you the gift to use your creations, your orbs, full potential, and see into them again. would you like to see your creations again??" the 7 all smiled and said yes. Hyperion lifted his other massive hand that wasn't still holding the 8 and pointed at them. a small glowing gold orb formed in front of them and shot a beam of light at their foreheads and dissipated into nothing leaving each their own colored gem in the middle of their forehead. They all gasped at the sudden wealth of knowledge left in their minds. They all immediately looked into their orbs to see what their creation was doing and to say Hello to their loved ones, except for Max.

Max started to truly cry for the first time tears of joy for a gift so precious to him. Max couldn't express the happiness he had that he could see Zoey and Jacob again, and was unable to control his emotions. Through wet eyes Max said to Hyperion "thank you Hyperion I have no idea how I'm going to repay you."

Hyperion smiled softly and said "take my request to be the first of my children to live with me and learn my knowledge."

Max trying calm himself down saying "yes, dad ill stay as long as you want"

Hyperion still smiling and with endless love tells Max "then look into your fathers creation and see the ones you love."

Max only nods and looks at his orb. A rush of air blast past Max's face. Then light. Then his body appears in front of their house in Colorado where the confused young Zoey and Jacob were already teleported to the spot by Max, stood. They see Max and run to him. Max grabs them into his embrace giving them each a kiss saying softly "I love you." –end scene